To those who inspired it

Eidolon (n): 1. An idealised person or thing.
2. A spectre or phantom

EIDOLON

SOFI CROFT

Published by Accent Press Ltd 2016

Paperback ISBN: 9781786151179
Ebook ISBN: 9781786150509

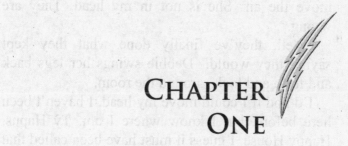

CHAPTER ONE

Before I even open my eyes my head starts spinning. I am both floating above and stuck fast to this bed. The sheet is damp with sweat but I'm cold. I cannot move. As light as my head is, it's too heavy to lift.

I open my eyes and a barcode of light and shadow races across my vision and I feel sick. I close my eyes and see Debbie, floating in the pit, her face frozen in a silent scream.

'Wakey wakey, Paul.'

I open my eyes again. She is sitting on a window ledge, running her hands across the vertical blinds. I squint as stripes of sunlight pierce my eyes and she laughs.

'Rough night, Paulie?'

1

I stare at her. They say she is not real.

She looks real to me.

If she is not real, how are the blinds moving? How is she casting a shadow? How can I hear her speak? I don't just hear her speak – I feel her voice move the air. She is not in my head. They are wrong.

'Well, they've finally done what they kept saying they would.' Debbie swings her legs back and forth and looks around the room.

I'd nod if I could move my head. I haven't been here before, but I know where I am. Tŷ Hapus. Happy House. I guess it must have been called that before it became what it is.

They've been threatening me with Tŷ Hapus for months. The police, the wardens, the case workers, the psychologists. They said I would end up here. If I did this or didn't do that. For a while I tried to figure out what they wanted me to do, but it didn't take long for me to realise I wasn't in control. I am not in control and I never have been.

Debbie turns back to me. 'Do you remember how you got here?'

I don't. I look at a crack in the wall and think back. The last thing I remember is being in my cell at young offenders. I remember the door opening. I remember a knee in my back, my face on the floor.

My head hurts. The spinning has stopped, but a throbbing has begun. Judging by how heavy my head is, by how bright the light is, they've drugged me. Again.

'They had to, Paul. They couldn't have moved you otherwise. You were awesome.' Debbie jumps off the ledge and punches the air. 'You should've seen what you did. One of them was so big he came through the door ducking and sideways, but you knocked him clean out with one punch. When you get out of here you'll be a fighter, Paulie. A champion.' Debbie smiles at me, eyes gleaming.

I don't remember hitting anyone. I never remember hitting anyone, not since that night in the pit. I try to move my hands to wipe the drool from my face, but they are trapped behind my back.

'Tŷ Hapus,' Debbie giggles. 'Happy House. Happy days.' She turns to me, and she goes all stiff and her eyes glaze over. Like they did in the pit. And she sings, slowly and quietly.

Oh happy day
Oh happy day
Oh when he washed
He washed my sins away.

She stares intently, through me, beyond me, at something far away. Something in another world.

Oh happy day
Oh happy day,

3

She sings faster, louder. She starts swaying, dancing.

Oh happy day
Oh happy day,

She is belting the song out now, in full gospel style. Her voice fills the room. Fills me. Her body is joyful, her voice is joyful, the song is joyful, but her eyes are dead. Just like in the pit.

Oh when he washed
Oh when he washed
When he washed
He washed my sins away,

Water surrounds her face and her hair floats up. Like it did in the pit.

Oh happy day
Oh happy day,

Something moves behind me and Debbie stops singing. I try to lift my head but give up almost instantly. I strain my eyes all the way to the left and make out a woman in a white coat behind a long window. Her thin, wrinkled face frowns and she walks away. I relax my eyes and Debbie is right of front of me.

Oh happy day
Oh happy day

Please, I think, please stop. My head hurts.

Even when I talk to Debbie inside my head she hears me. Does that mean she is inside my head, like they say? I look at her and she looks back at me. She is so real. Her eyes are filled with all the emotion they carried in life. Excitement. Fear. Anger. Sadness. Every emotion apart from happiness. Apart from joy. She could always sing joyful, but she could never be joyful.

'Poor Paulie,' she smiles and strokes my hair, 'too loud for you?'

If she is not real, how do I feel her hand? It is cool, soothing. I close my eyes. She hums the next verse softly, but the words form in my head anyway.

When he washed
Oh when he washed
When he washed my sins away.

Please stop, I think. Please.

Her hand disappears. Her song disappears. Her breath disappears. The air that moved with her is now still.

I squeeze my eyes shut but a tear still escapes. I grunt with the effort it takes to drag my face across the sheet to rub it away.

Metal slides against metal and the door heaves open. Footsteps approach my bed and I open my eyes. The woman in the white coat is flanked by two enormous men in blue overalls. They look strong, but slow. I stare one of the buffalo in the eye and he looks away. I could take him. I look the other one in the eye. He stares back but folds his fat arms across his chest. I could take them both; if I had to.

I remember I can barely move my head. My arms are trapped behind me and I can't even feel my legs. What have they done to me?

The woman flicks through her notes. 'Ogaji, Paul.' She lifts her head and looks me in the eye. 'I'm Dr Stuart.' There is something hard about her. I can't help it. I look away.

'Welcome to Tŷ Hapus, Paul. Do you understand why you're here?'

I understand. They want to take Debbie away.

'This is a small, specialised unit for special cases such as yourself.'

This is where they send you when there is nowhere left to send you.

'You are here to be treated for your psychosis, Paul. You have already been assessed and diagnosed. That is not my job. My job is to find the right medications to control your condition. It can be a difficult process, but we will persevere until we find a solution.'

'I don't want medication.' The bed muffles my voice. I've been given medication before. It doesn't help. It makes it worse.

Dr Stuart taps a pen on her clipboard. 'This is a necessary course of action for your safety and the safety of others. Attempts to treat you without medication have been unsuccessful.' She flicks back through her notes. 'You have been uncommunicative, aggressive and violent.'

Anger flushes through me and I clench my fists. I just didn't want to talk about Debbie. They kept saying she wasn't real, that she was in my head. They wanted to know when I saw her, what she said to me. They wanted to talk about that night in the pit, when she died. I didn't.

'I understand previous attempts at medicating may not have helped but we have access to highly specialised drugs here, things you won't have tried before. We will find the right medications.'

I turn to Dr Stuart. I look her right in the eye, and say as firmly and calmly as I can, 'I refuse medication.'

She stares back at me and frowns. 'That is not possible, Paul. I'm sorry.'

She's not sorry.

'These gentlemen will take care of your personal needs. I will see you later today to begin treatment.' She turns and walks to the door.

I am alone with the buffalo. Before I have a chance to say or do anything, one of them takes a step forward and puts his hand on the back of my head, pressing my face into the bed until I can barely breathe. I feel the other one fiddling with straps on my back. I hear tape tearing and I feel air on my hand. I move my fingers and he grabs them, holds my hand still. A needle pierces my skin. A warm sensation spreads up from the back of my hand, and I am warm all over, and everything is soft. The buffalo start to talk. Not to me. To each other. About the football. They seem far away.

My head is released and I feel them lifting me up. I try to struggle but my limbs are lifeless. What follows is humiliating. They half carry, half drag me to a toilet in the corner of the room. They undo straps, pull at clothes, and prop me up, all the while talking about football. I can't focus. What have they done to me?

I am face down on the bed again. They are loosening the straps. They have released my arms. I love them. I don't want to, but I love those buffalo men. My feet hit the bed and I love them even more. The buffalo have freed me. I am free. I could stand up and knock them out and run away. I could if I wanted to. I will do, later. I am just so comfortable right now, sinking into this bed.

CHAPTER TWO

A door is kicked open. Not my door. Debbie's. In the old house, the bungalow, where we lived when I was six and she was nine. Where Mum died. My father grumbles something in the incoherent way he does after he's been drinking. I don't know what Debbie says, but I can hear fear in her voice in the way she tries to act calm and strong and unconcerned when she feels the opposite.

There is a scuffle and a thud. Then the crying starts. The pleading. Fear seeps through the wall between us. I bury my head under my pillow and squeeze my eyes shut and pray, but it doesn't go away.

Banging. Screaming. Shouting. A whimper. A sob. Something heavy falls over and smashes. I wrap my arms over my pillow and pull it tight around my ears and moan, loud enough to block out the noise, but quiet enough that he doesn't hear me.

Hate wells up like bile in my throat. Not hate for him. Hate for me, because I am doing nothing. Hiding under a pillow, pretending I can't hear. I smell the fear, sharp and stale. It suffocates me. I lift my head and take a breath.

Shaking, I slide my feet to the floor and creep silently to the window. I lift the latch and push it open and the smell of fear floats into the night air. I climb out and run to the front of the house, bare toes on the concrete path, and bang on the door, three times, as loud as my tiny fists can manage. And I run.

I hear Debbie's door slam shut. He shouts something, a slurred warning to stay where she is, and he lumbers through the house like a buffalo. A minute. It will take him a minute to open the door, maybe two. All the time we need. I tap softly, persistently, on Debbie's window. Seconds ticking by. Please open the window. Please.

A curtain slides back. Her face is red and wet and puffy and her arms are crossed over her body tight. She opens the window with one hand. She climbs out and pulls the curtain shut, slowly lowers the latch, and grabs my hand and we run.

Along the concrete path to the back of the house, across the wet, muddy grass, through the gap in the fence and into the woods. Over sharp sticks and cold stones, slippery tree roots and prickly leaves. The orange glow of the streetlights disappears behind the thickening canopy. We don't speak. We barely breathe. We just run and walk and stumble, holding hands tight. Her pink dressing gown trails behind us like a cape, darkening to red the further we go, then grey, then black.

I hear him and freeze. Debbie stops in her tracks and squeezes my hand. His shout rolls across the air like drunken, sleepy thunder. He is far away.

'He won't follow us,' Debbie whispers.

We remain still. I listen for his footfalls. The sounds of the night envelope us. Silence. Just wind on the air.

I step forward and pull Debbie's hand. 'Let's go,' I whisper.

'Where?' Debbie stands firm, like a statue.

'Let's run away,' I pull her forward but she doesn't budge.

She looks around and I follow her gaze. Tall, black trees surround us. The dark sky is hidden beyond a tangle of empty branches.

'There is nowhere to go, Paulie,' she says simply. 'We'll wait here. He'll be different in the morning.' She lifts me onto a fallen tree, sits beside me, and pulls her dressing gown around us both. She wraps her arms around me and starts humming, like Mum used to.

I lift my feet onto the tree and pull them close to

my body. The hems of my pyjama trousers are wet and muddy. Tiny supermen are flying through the mud. They are strong, determined, fists raised as they fly.

'I'll be strong one day, Debbie, and I'll protect you from him.'

Debbie keeps on humming, rocking me gently back and forth until I fall asleep.

CHAPTER THREE

Debbie is humming. I open my eyes. Whatever drugs they gave me have worn off. I sit up and look at her. She is on the window ledge again, strumming the blinds. I'm not crazy. I know she is dead. I just don't believe she is only in my head. She has presence. I think she might be a ghost. Lots of people believe in ghosts, and they aren't crazy.

'That's a matter of opinion,' Debbie laughs.

Mum believed in ghosts.

'Mum believed in God.'

What's that got to do with it?

'Same nonsense.'

Don't say that. You used to believe in God.

'That was before.' Debbie looks out of the window and starts humming again.

Oh happy day.

So what are you if you're not a ghost?

'I'm in your head.'

You're messing with my head.

Debbie laughs and jumps off the window ledge. 'It never took much to confuse you, did it, Paulie?'

Why would you want to?

'Spar with me, Paul.' She jumps around, punching the air in front of my face.

'No.' I say it out loud. I hate it when she wants to fight.

'Oh, come *on*, Paul. You need to stay in shape or you'll go flabby like those buffalo.'

Why do you always want to fight me?

'To punish you.'

I frown. I feel cold.

'I'm *joking*, Paul. Come *on*.'

I stand up. She backs away from me a little. I stretch and breathe. I turn to her again. She is still punching the air.

Why are you here?

'You know.'

No, I don't.

'I'm here to help you, Paulie. I'm going to help you to be strong, to be a fighter.' She starts humming again.

Oh happy day
Oh happy day.

She sings the words, still boxing the air.

Oh happy day
Oh happy day
Oh happy day
Oh happy day
When he washed
When he washed
He washed my sins away
I taught him to fight
I taught him to pray
I taught him to fight and I taught him to pray
Oh happy day.

Debbie did teach me to fight. I got strong to protect her. But I couldn't. Didn't.

She taught me to pray, too. I used to go to church to hear her sing. Then I went to pray for her. To pray for me. Sometimes I even prayed for Dad; I prayed the devil would take him away. I never prayed for Mum, though. It was too late for her.

Do you see Mum?

'Mum's dead.'

So are you.

'And you think that makes us best mates now?' Debbie raises her eyebrows to the window behind me, 'Look, you're being watched.'

I turn around. Dr Stuart is behind the glass, frowning. She writes something on a clipboard and walks away.

Debbie moves to the window, presses her hands and forehead against it, and her breath clouds the glass. That wouldn't happen if she was only in my head.

'Come and see, Paulie.'

I walk towards her. I can smell her hair, the shampoo she always used. I want to reach out and touch her, but I can't. Something always stops me. I look away, out of the window. It faces a wall. Debbie points along the corridor. I lean against the window and look as far to the left as I can. There is another window opposite, further along the corridor. I see shapes moving behind the glass. There are people in there. Not just one person, but people. All wearing yellow overalls, like me.

One of them stands and walks to the window. He presses his face against it, looks right at me, and smiles broadly. He smiles like a child on a waterslide, eyes bright, excited. But he is nearly a man. Like me. He looks Hispanic, or maybe Native American. I nod to him and he raises his hand. He breathes on the glass and writes the letter C. He breathes again and writes R. He carries on like this until he has spelled out CRAZY HORSE, then he waves a hand above his head and gallops off into the room behind him. I imagine him screaming some kind of war cry as he goes.

16

'Crazy Horse looks fun.' Debbie walks back to her ledge. 'I wonder if they'll let you go and play.'

I turn to Debbie and, as I do, I see a man out of the corner of my eye walking past the window behind me. He is dressed like a Native American chief, a huge feathered headdress sitting on top of his head, held high. I turn back to the window but there is no one there.

Perhaps I *am* crazy, like they say. They use different words of course; schizophrenic, paranoid, delusional. Long words that mean I'm crazy, losing my mind.

I sit on the bed and look around the room; a toilet, a sink, pale green walls, white floor tiles cracked and yellowed with age. Oh happy day.

'You haven't looked at the view yet.' Debbie pushes the blinds apart. I have a view of the outside world. Trees. Lots of them. And in the distance, the ocean. I imagine getting out of here, running through the woods and reaching the sea. Would there be a beach? A harbour? Maybe I could find a boat and we could sail away, me and Debbie. I could save her this time.

Panic rises in my chest. They want to take her away. That's why they sent me here, to get rid of her. They are going to drug me, give me medicines that mess with my mind. Medicines that take her away. I need to get out of here. I can't lose her again.

I fall to the floor and start doing press ups. I'll

take them out. The buffalo. I'll take them out and I'll run away, run away with Debbie like I should have done before.

CHAPTER FOUR

The sun is blazing, the sky too bright to look at. A green door is propped open with a high stool. It's a fire door, the long, metal panic bar shining in the light. Noises float out of the building into the heavy summer air. Thumps and grunts and shouts. Skipping ropes smacking the floor. I hold the strap of my school bag tight and I walk to the door, palms sweating.

It's dark inside and I take my sunglasses off, forgetting about the bruises. A couple of faces turn to me and look away. No one says anything. They carry on with what they're doing; some are lifting weights, some skipping, some punching bags. Most are gathered around the square platform in the centre of the gym watching two men jump around each other, boxing gloves raised in front of their faces.

A man with a towel over his shoulder walks towards me. He is short and stocky, with fuzzy white hair. His eyebrows rise in a question. I twist the strap of the school bag in my hands. 'I'd like to learn boxing.' My voice is a whisper.

The man tilts his head and looks at my face. 'How old are you?'

'Ten,' I lie.

'Do you do any sports?'

'At school.'

The man wipes his face with the towel. 'Best thing you can do at your age is as many sports as possible. Lots of variety. You can learn boxing when you're older.'

My hands slip on the strap. 'I'd like to learn boxing. Please.'

'This isn't a club for children. Have you been to the leisure centre to see what classes they offer?'

I look at the floor. I have no money for classes, and I know they don't offer boxing.

'You can start training here when you're fourteen. In the meantime, do as many sports as you can. OK, lad?' He reaches up, probably to grab his towel again, but I flinch.

The man leans down and nods at my face. 'How did that happen?'

'I fell off my bike.'

I don't have a bike.

'Snowy!' Someone shouts from the side of the

ring. The man glances over and holds up a hand, then turns back to me.

'Tell you what,' the man sighs and wipes his face again, 'come here at four tomorrow with your gym kit, and I'll show you some exercises you can practice at home.'

I nod and run back into the heat and light of the summer sun. I run all the way home, hiding a great smile of hope.

CHAPTER FIVE

There is a light so bright I feel its heat. I try to turn my head away but it is held fast. A strap presses down on my forehead, another on my chin. I panic and struggle to move my limbs. I feel straps on my wrists, my chest, my legs. I hear a groan and it takes me a moment to realise it's coming from me.

How did I get here? I ache all over, feel sore and bruised. Did I fight? I never remember fighting. Not since that night.

Debbie?

I can't hear her, can't feel her presence. No air is moving, no breeze.

'He's coming round.'

'Is he secure?' Dr Stuart. I'm sure that's Dr Stuart.

The straps pull tighter.

Someone is messing with my hair, squashing it,

trying to pull something over my head.

'The cap won't fit over his hair.'

'Cut it off,' Dr Stuart orders.

Scissors crunch around my head.

The hacking stops and a rubbery cap slaps onto my scalp.

A shadow blocks the light and I open my eyes. Dr Stuart has wires in her hands. She attaches them to the cap. I fight. With every muscle in my body I fight but I can't break free. I can barely move.

'Relax, Paul.' Dr Stuart is focused on attaching the wires to my head. 'The machine simply monitors your reaction to different medications. It's a painless procedure.'

I keep fighting. I focus on my hands. If I can get my hands free...

Dr Stuart leans back and I have to close my eyes again. The light is bright, even through my eyelids.

'Prep 1.'

A hand grabs my hand and injects me with something. Cold forces its way into the veins on the back of my hand. It flows up my arms, down my legs, washes over my face. I open my eyes but the light is still too bright and I close them again.

'I refuse medication.' I force the words out of my lips, jammed together by the strap on my chin.

'Prep 2.'

The buffalo injects cold into my hand again and water runs over my body. The light dims. I open my eyes. Debbie is floating near the ceiling. Eyes glazed like in the pit. My eyes sting and I blink fast. I won't cry.

I hear a roar. My chin hurts. My forehead hurts. I am roaring. Good. If I keep roaring, the power of it will snap the restraints. My roar will short circuit the wires. My roar will ... but I need to breathe. I stop roaring.

Dr Stuart sighs.

I open my eyes. Debbie is there. I close my eyes. I still see her.

'A.'

The buffalo squeezes my fingers and injects warm. Everything slows down; my thoughts, my heart, my breathing. Panic ebbs away. I don't want it to be nice, but it is. I open my eyes and Debbie is gone. I hear her humming across the room. I try to turn to her, but the straps stop me.

'I'm here, Paulie.'

Help me, Debbie. You said you were here to help me.

'And I will, Paul. I will help you.'

Dr Stuart flicks through her papers and writes something down.

'B.'

The buffalo injects hot. It burns its way up my arm, down my legs. My veins are going to burst. My *VEINS* are going to *BURST*. I roar again. I roar so loud my ears hurt. My *VEINS* are going to *BURST* and my *EARDRUMS* are going to *RUPTURE*.

HE TAUGHT ME TO FIGHT.

Debbie sings louder than my roar. I stop and listen to her.

AND HE TAUGHT ME TO PRAY
HE TAUGHT ME TO FIGHT AND HE
TAUGHT ME TO PRAY
OH HAPPY DAY.

I let her voice fill me.

Oh happy day

'C.'
The buffalo injects magma into my hand and it turns my blood to steam. The blood steam rushes round my body and the magma creeps along my veins, turning them to ash. They crumble into my muscles, making them weak. I clench my teeth, my jaw.

OH HAPPY DAY.

I stare at the ceiling and count. I will count, and at some point this will stop. I count to ten, and I count to ten, over and over and over.
'D.'
Glue. It makes my blood thicken and slow. My

26

heart has to beat harder to pump it round my body. I hear it slowing under the weight of my blood. My chest pounds, my ears ache. I can't hear Debbie. Debbie?

'I'm here, Paul.' She is far away. I search the ceiling.

'E.'

No, I think. No more. *Please.* I squeeze my eyes shut. I won't cry.

E is spiders. They wriggle through my veins and crawl across my skin. I want to brush them away but I can't.

F is rocks that crash down veins, smash through blood vessels, bruise my arms and legs. I count. I breathe. At some point this will stop.

'G.'

I blink. I breathe. I will get through this.

'No, wait,' Dr Stuart rises, looks into my eyes and frowns. She sighs and looks away, to the buffalo. 'We're done.'

Relief flows over me like a cool breeze, but it feeds flames of anger underneath and I end up burning, shaking, sweating.

'Give him prep 3 and a sedative, and take him for a shower.' Dr Stuart walks away.

Debbie?

I can't hear her.

Cold pierces my hand, washes over me; cools and revives me. My heart stops pounding.

'I'm here, Paul.'

Where did you go?

'I was here. You just couldn't hear me.'

We have to get out of here.

One of the buffalo slides the cap from my head and releases the straps on my forehead and chin. I stare at the ceiling, clenching my jaw. I have to fight. I have to escape.

Another injection. It's the one that makes me warm and makes everything soft and comfortable. It's the one that takes away my will and my strength, but I'll still fight. I'll still beat them. I have to get out of here.

The buffalo unfasten all the straps but I still can't move my limbs; they are heavy, useless. They peel off my overalls, soaked with sweat. They lift me, the buffalo, two of them. They lift me and tie my hands behind my back. I am cold, naked and bound, but I'll still fight them. I'll still beat them. I try to clench my fists.

They drag me out, along a corridor, through a door, and into a room that is freezing. My body shivers uncontrollably and they drop me onto the floor, against a wall. I rest my head against the cold tiles and try to keep my eyes open, try to focus.

Pipes rattle and clang and the showers come on; fat, cold drops of water hammer onto my face. I stare through the rain and focus on the buffalo. There are two of them, leaning against a wall, just a few steps away.

I tense all my muscles and push myself up. I stand, stagger towards them, and they look up and I run, hurtle towards them, and throw myself into them …

I am on my knees, cold and wet and naked. Blood, diluted by water, is streaming towards a drain. My hands are tied behind my back and my head hurts. The buffalo are on the floor, unconscious; one on his back, one on his front. I don't remember how they got like that. I never remember.

I stand up and my head spins. I slip and slide to the door, push my way through. I zigzag down the corridor. I keep slipping, falling. Everything is spinning and black dots cloud my vision.

Debbie?

'I'm here, Paul.'

Which way?

'You're naked, Paul.'

I know. Which way?

'Your hands are tied behind your back.'

I KNOW.

'What are you doing?'

I have to get out of here.

'I know you do. But now? Like this? Have you thought this through?'

SHUT UP! Help me!

'This isn't going to work, Paul, not this time.'

SHUT UP. I have to get of here. *RIGHT NOW*.

I run, faster and faster, along the corridor, around a corner, through some doors.

'Paul, you're naked. Your arms are tied.'

I KNOW. SHUT UP.

Clothes don't matter. Arms don't matter. Getting out is all that matters. The doors ahead are metal, but I can see stairs through a small window on them. Stairs are good; down is out. I slam into the doors but they don't give; they're locked.

I charge the doors, barge them, kick them. They shake, rattle and dent, but they won't give. They won't open. They have to open. I kick and kick, ignoring the pain that it brings. An alarm sounds; the wail drowns out the noise of me beating the doors, but still I hear Debbie.

'Your arms are tied and you're naked and those doors are locked, Paulie.'

SHUT UP, DEBBIE. I am going to get out of here. We are going to get out of here.

I kick and kick and kick. My foot throbs and numbs and my leg aches and my eyes well up and I can't see, but I keep kicking. I beat the doors harder and harder, but they won't open. They're breaking me, and they still won't open.

CHAPTER SIX

'Rough night, Paulie?'

I am face down on the bed again. My arms are trapped behind my back. I can't move my legs and I ache all over. I am sore, swollen, stiff, bruised, thirsty and angry. I feel the sharp twinge of stitches above my eye. My head feels cold and I remember they cut my hair.

'Do you remember fighting?'

I don't remember fighting. Not since ... My eyes sting and I blink, fast.

'Your hands were tied and you still took them down. There were two in the shower; you charged them like a bull, knocked them into a wall. They didn't know what hit them. You head-butted one, leg swiped the other. They fell like sacks of bricks, smashed into the floor. Then in the corridor...'

I remember the corridor, the door between

me and the stairs.

'It took four of them to take you down, and each one of them got some. All the buffalo have bruises today. Two have stitches. One is in hospital. You were awesome.'

Why didn't you help me?

Debbie strums the blinds and starts humming.

The door heaves open and footsteps approach. Two buffalo. They work in silence, unfastening straps, pulling at clothes, dragging me to the toilet, then back to the bed, refastening straps. All the while one of them pushes my head down into my chest. I think about fighting them. The right moment will come, and I will get out of here. We will get out of here, together.

The door opens again and another buffalo walks in. A woman. She is big, solid like a great rock. She looks at the buffalo holding my head down and he lets go.

'You're needed in Ward B. I'll take over here.'

The buffalo grunts and leaves, and the woman turns to me. She looks at me, hard and unyielding, for an uncomfortably long time, but then her face cracks and she laughs, 'O Lord in Heaven, what have they done to your hair, child?'

'I know her,' Debbie says from the window ledge. 'She was in my choir.'

I look up at the woman. 'You knew my sister?'

She goes all hard again and touches the remaining buffalo on the arm. 'Go and get some hair clippers.'

'You can't be alone with him.'

'He isn't going to fight me. Are you, Paul?' She looks at me, and I look away.

'It's on the sheets, Pam.'

'Shush. Go and get some clippers.'

He crosses his arms over his chest.

Pam leans towards him, 'Give me ten minutes. You can lock us in.'

The buffalo shifts his weight. 'Ten minutes. Sedate him.'

'I'm not daft; I don't want a face like yours.'

It's then I notice the buffalo's face is all beaten up; swollen and bruised. Did I do that?

The door closes and locks. Pam looks at me and furrows her brow. 'I was going to punch you, Paul, but I can see someone's already done that.' She grabs my chin and lifts it, inspects my face. 'I guess it's not my place to punish you, anyway. The good Lord will do that.'

Is that what this is? Punishment?

'You remember me from church, Paul?' She releases my chin. 'I did know your sister. And your mother. I met your father a couple of times, too. He's the reason I'm here.'

The blinds move. Debbie has gone.

'No one has told you, have they?' She searches my face and shakes her head. 'I knew they wouldn't. Shame on them.' She sits next to me and the bed groans. 'He's dead, Paul.'

Dead.

I feel frustrated, angry. The timing is all wrong. He should have died years ago. Before he ... and I should have...

'He got into a fight in the prison he was in, and didn't come out of it. I thought you should know.'

We both sit there for a while, staring at the blinds. They don't move. Debbie is not here. I wonder if she knows. I wonder if she is happy. Or angry, like me.

'It's not wrong to think of it as a blessing, Paul. He was a wicked man.' She takes a deep breath. 'You know and I know and the good Lord knows what killed your sister.'

I feel cold. My eyes sting.

'Part of your sister died years before that night.' She takes another deep breath and straightens her back. 'What happened that night was wrong, and there has to be a penance for that, but the good Lord knows that is not what killed your sister. You've got to move on.' She lifts her hand like she's going to put it on my shoulder, but she doesn't. It just hovers in the air between us for a moment before she lowers it back to the bed. 'The good Lord works in mysterious ways, child. You remember that,' she looks around the room, 'especially while you're in here. I believe He has a plan for you, Paul. He has a plan for all of us.'

I am going to break out of here. That's my plan. Me and Debbie, together.

The door opens. The buffalo has returned with clippers. He passes them to Pam and she stands up.

'Right, Paul, let's sort out this patchy mess on your head.' She looks me in the eye. 'Do I have to sedate you?'

I shake my head. I won't fight Pam. She knew Debbie, sang with her; her presence makes me feel closer to Debbie somehow.

'Good, because I hate beating up boys.'

The clippers buzz and she starts to hum.

Oh happy day
Oh happy day.

Debbie's voice joins hers and soon they are singing together, and their voices are powerful, so powerful I might break. I have to tense all my muscles to keep from falling apart.

Oh happy day
Oh happy day
Oh happy day
Oh happy day
When Jesus washed
When Jesus washed
When Jesus washed
Oh when He washed
He washed my sins away
Oh happy day
Happy day

The clippers stop buzzing and she sweeps the hair from my head, my shoulders. 'That was her favourite song.' Pam's hand lingers on my shoulder. 'She sang so sweetly.'

I glance at her and see tears in her eyes. I look away.

'Do you sing, Paul?'

I shake my head.

'They sing here sometimes, on the wards; play music, create art, read books, play games. It's not all bad, you know. If you stop fighting like a caged animal they might move you to a ward. You've just got to settle down, accept your fate. Let them help you. Here is where you have to be right now. It's not forever.'

'What they do … the treatment …' I want to say what they did last night, with the restraints, and the wires and the injections. That can't be right. Can it?

'I know it can be difficult, especially at the start, but it will get easier, and it will help. You'll see. Everything happens for a reason.'

The other buffalo returns with a tray of food; he puts it on my bed and nods to Pam.

'You must be hungry.' Pam moves to the door. 'Remember, we're all here to help, Paul. It's easier if you don't fight us.'

The door locks and I am alone again. I look at the food. I am hungry. I start to eat when a buffalo walks past the window, along the corridor. He is followed by patients, all in yellow overalls like mine. There are two girls; one with long, dark hair, and the other with very short, fair hair, like it was all shaved off not too long ago. Then there are two boys; an older boy, with wide, startled eyes, and a younger boy with bright red hair. The last boy is bald, with fresh, raw scars all over his head and wires poking out through them.

I have to get out of here.

I press my forehead to the window and watch the patients file into the ward. Pam arrives at the door from the other direction, wheeling a trolley full of paper and paints.

Maybe if I get on a ward it will be easier to escape.

'Now you're thinking, Paul. You're not as dumb as you look.'

Shut up.

'Well, you're not known for your smarts, are you?'

Shut up.

'It doesn't matter. I'll be the brain, you be the brawn.'

SHUT UP.

Debbie jumps off the window ledge and boxes the air. 'Spar with me, Paul.'

I ignore her and look at the blinds. Maybe there is something I can use as a skipping rope. There is no string, no cord, and the blinds themselves are paper thin.

'See what I mean, Paul?'

What?

'You don't think. Why would they leave something like a rope here for you?'

OK, that was stupid. I start skipping with an imaginary rope.

'Spar with me, Paul.'

No.

Her hair bounces as she jumps around. Light and shadows play on her face. She is so real. How can that be?

Oh happy day.

I think of Pam, singing with her.

Can other people hear you, Debbie?

'I'm in your head, Paulie.' She throws a jab and her arm catches the skipping rope; I feel it pull my hands.

But there is no rope. And there is no Debbie. Debbie died in the pit.

'I'm here, Paul.' She gently puts her fingers on my hand. They feel warm. They feel real. My eyes sting and I blink fast. I fall to the floor and do press ups. I do press ups and I count to ten, over and over and over. I keep doing them until my overalls are soaked with sweat, until it is dripping off my forehead and pooling on the floor and my muscles are burning like they are on fire.

I stop and listen for Debbie. It is silent, still; no

air is moving, no breeze. She is not here. I am alone. I stand, lean against the corridor window and look down to the ward. Crazy Horse is at the window. He smiles when he sees me and writes in his breath, SAVE HER.

Save who? Debbie? He would have no way of knowing about Debbie, would he? Why am I trying to make sense of what he writes, anyway? I guess he's in here because he's crazy. Like me.

ESCAPE, he writes.

I nod. That's the plan.

BRING THE WIND, he writes.

It makes no sense. He would have no way of knowing. He is crazy. I'm not going to try to make sense of him.

I don't get a chance anyway, because the door opens and I turn to see buffalo filing into the room.

CHAPTER SEVEN

I am in the ring, sweating, my heart pounding, watching my opponent from behind my gloves. He drops his guard to throw a punch and I duck out of the way and jab. I keep attacking, moving towards him as he backs away, blocking and reeling. A straight right, a left hook, a right hook, a left uppercut, a right uppercut, and another hook connects with the side of his head and he falls to the floor; the referee steps between us.

I breathe hard. My blood is surging around my body, my head is light, and I feel sick. The referee grabs my hand and lifts it over my head. Snowy appears next to me. He holds my head and slaps my back. A camera flashes and I panic. There can't be photos. I don't want him to find out. I scramble from the ring and jog back to the changing rooms.

Debbie takes my gloves off. She is smiling,

beaming. 'You were awesome, Paulie. You did it. You're a champion.'

Snowy walks in carrying a trophy that looks like a brass boxing glove. 'Youngest under fourteen champion, ever. You did well, lad. The local paper wants a picture.'

I shake my head.

We walk home, me and Debbie, together. She talks about choir and singing and auditions for a show she will never be allowed to participate in. She talks about boxing and competitions and big prize money. We slow as we turn the corner. The block of flats looms ahead. Silently we climb the stairs and silently we pause outside the door, listening.

It's quiet. He might not be home.

Debbie turns the key and steps inside.

It's quiet. He might not be home.

She walks through the corridor to the kitchen, and I follow, pausing outside his door.

It's quiet. He might not be home.

He's slumped over the kitchen table.

My heart sinks. He's home.

He lifts his head and stares at me. It takes him a moment to focus, then his eyes narrow. 'I know where you've been, boy.'

'What?' I say calmly, like maybe I didn't hear what he said. Like I am not concerned. I smell the fear seeping through my skin and I hate myself for it.

'You want to fight? You want to be a tough guy?' He sways to his feet, steps out from behind the table and lifts his fists in front of his body. 'Let's see it then.'

I stare at him, wide eyed. He is enormous. A tower of hard muscle looking down at me, eyes cloudy with the drink.

'I said let's see it. Show me what you've learned. Show me your stance. Try and hit me.'

'Dad,' Debbie steps between us and he pushes her out of the way with one of his giant hands. She stumbles sideways and backs away.

'I wasn't talking to you, girl. Go to your room.' He looks straight at me. His eyebrows fall and he glares at me, his jaw tense and his temple pulsing. 'Who gave you permission to go there?'

'It's just a club. For sports. For fitness.' My voice wavers. I hate myself for it.

'It's a boxing club. Do you think I'm stupid, boy?' He lurches towards me, grabbing a handful of my skin and clothes and he swings me to the floor. My hands fly up around my head and I curl into a ball like I always do. I hate myself.

I think about the jabs and the hooks and the uppercuts I was throwing just an hour before. I think about standing up and knocking him to the floor with a superhuman punch but I can't move. I am just a tight ball of fear.

I hear Debbie pleading with him. He ignores her. He is lost in drunken anger, shouting at me, punching me. I can't hear the words and I can barely feel the blows. I am detached from it all, trapped in a hard, tense box, blood pounding in my ears.

When he starts kicking I feel it. In my ribs, my head. Impact after impact smashes me into pieces until I can't breathe. I can't think. I squeeze my eyes shut and wait for it to stop but it goes on forever, cycles of collision and pain. Bruises throb and blood vessels burst, nerve ending fire across wounds like lightning. He kicks me, again and again, and I lie there unmoving, weak and useless, until all there is the moment before the kick and the kick. I focus on the blood, pounding, stinging the back of my eyes until everything is quiet and dark.

Lights flash through my eyelids. They coalesce into the shape of a tunnel and I open my eyes. My father is gone. I try and lift my head but it is too heavy. It rolls to the side and I see him. He looks far away, like I'm looking at him through the wrong end of a telescope. He is collapsed on the floor, his head in his hands. He's sobbing, tears and drool dribbling down his face. A high-pitched whine fills the air between us. I don't know if it's him, or me, or just a noise in my ears.

I roll all the way over and get onto my knees. I let go of my head and push off from the floor. Blood drips onto the grey carpet. Stain on stain.

'Debbie.' My voice is a gurgle. A whisper.

I crawl to her room, pitching sideways, my head so heavy it pulls my whole body down. I knock on her door. A soft, persistent tap. The chest of drawers slides out of the way behind the door and she pulls me in. We push the drawers back across the door and the bed, too. I lie down and stare out of window of our eighth floor flat and I miss the bungalow and the woods behind it.

CHAPTER EIGHT

Cold water washes over me and I wake. I close my eyes against the bright light and strain against the straps holding me down.

Not here.

Not again.

'Relax, Paul.' Dr Stuart leans over me and clips a wire to my head. 'This won't take long. We made good progress yesterday. Hopefully, by the end of this session, we'll know what medications to start you on.'

'I don't want –'

'You need medication.' Dr Stuart looks me in the eye and frowns. 'You see your sister, don't you, Paul?' She doesn't wait for an answer. 'You have blackouts, memory problems. Delusions. These are all symptoms of your illness, caused by irregular brain activity. If we don't treat you, your condition will deteriorate.' She clips another wire to my head. 'You are lucky, Paul. We test the newest, most advanced medicines here. We will not only find the right treatment for you, but the results of our experiments will help many others with conditions like yours.'

I hear Debbie on the other side of the room. 'They want to get rid of me, Paul. Don't let them get rid of me.'

I won't. We are going to get out of here. We are going to get out of here together.

A door swings open and light footsteps approach. A man in a white coat leans over me. His face is in shadow but I see a kind, sympathetic smile. 'Hello, Paul, I'm Dr Epstein. I work in another one of our facilities, but I'll be observing today.' His face disappears and I hear a chair pull up close. 'What's the baseline activity?'

'580.' Dr Stuart flicks through her papers. 'Activity was 640 yesterday on arrival, two further readings of 540 and 560 under sedation.'

'Does he project?'

'Possible occurrences in the young offenders' institution he came from. Highly likely, but as yet unconfirmed.'

'How did he respond yesterday?'

Dr Stuart turns a page, 'Prep 1, 50 % activity; prep 2, 100%; A, 80%; B, 110%; C, 105%; D, 30%; E, 20%; F, 10%; prep 3, 95%.'

'How are you proceeding?'

'Prep 1 has been administered, activity at 57%. I plan to increase activity with prep 2, then repeat B and F – the high and low – to increase then decrease activity.'

'Proceed.'

'Prep 2.'

A buffalo grabs my hand and injects cold. The light dims and I open my eyes. Debbie is floating near the ceiling, eyes glazed like in the pit. I call to her but she doesn't respond. Anger builds inside me. If enough anger builds I could break these restraints, I'm sure I could.

'92%.'

'Proceed.'

'B.'

The buffalo injects hot. It sears through my veins. I clench my fists, I squeeze my eyes shut. I see Debbie sparring, singing.

I TAUGHT HIM TO FIGHT
AND I TAUGHT HIM TO FIGHT.

She taught me to fight. I'm not letting her go.

I'm not letting you go.

'They can't get rid of me, Paul. I am stronger than them.'

'117%.'

'Proceed.'

'F.'

Rocks fall from the ceiling and I lose Debbie. She's trapped under them. I'm trapped under them.

I try to push them off me, try to wriggle through the cracks. I can't breathe, they are crushing me. They must be crushing Debbie too. Debbie?

I hear a low groan, far, far away.

'12%.'

'Don't let them get rid of me, Paul.'

I won't. We are going to get out of here together.

'Restart.'

'Prep 2.'

Cold water hits me. Air bursts into my lungs. Debbie?

'I'm here, Paul.'

'96%.'

'G.'

Everything goes black. I am floating on black, warm water. I breathe slowly. This is nice.

Debbie?

'Paul?' She sounds sleepy, far away.

'60%, 30%.'

I reach out to her but she is drifting away.

'10%, 5%, holding steady.'

'H.'

I'm in space. I see stars, nebula. The universe is beautiful.

A faint breeze. A whisper on the wind. I look down. There is a small, round lake, far below, surrounded by steep cliffs. I think it's called the pit.

'3%, 2%, 1%, holding steady.'

It is quiet, dark. I'm not sure why I'm here. I think I was looking for someone.

'Excellent. That's enough, I think. Plan for tomorrow?'

'Allow activity to increase as much as possible during the day, then confirm the effectiveness of H.'

'Have you enough security measures in place?'

'Yes.'

'The Director is concerned.'

'We can handle him.'

'Are you sure? I could take him to Tŷ Eidolon now.'

'I haven't finished my investigations.'

I drift off. I was looking for someone, but I can't remember who, and I have to think, I have to remember who it was.

CHAPTER NINE

I am walking through the woods, looking for Debbie. The sun is setting. Orange light and long shadows. I need to find her before dark. She always comes here when she is sad or angry or hurt. When it's all too much she comes here. To the woods behind our old house, the bungalow where mum died. Through the woods and to the pit.

I climb over the low barbed wire fence and cross the field of scrubby yellow grass. The sun is behind me and my shadow extends in front of me, all the way to the cliff edge. The sky is a heavy blue, pressing down on my forehead and eyelids.

The path down the cliffs is steep and narrow, the small, round lake directly below. There are no plants, no roots. Just sheer rock. I see her ahead, sitting in our spot; the ledge that overlooks the pit. She is in the far corner of the small platform, leaning against the cliff wall, knees up to her chest.

'Debbie?'

'Leave me alone.'

I sit next to her and reach out and put my hand on her shoulder. 'Please, Debbie.'

'Please what?' She lifts her head and glares at me. Her eyes are red and sore. Her face is hard with anger and pain. I hate it when she is like this.

'Come home with me.'

'No.' She stares straight ahead, her eyes burning.

'I'll protect you.' In this moment I believe I will. I believe I can.

'You can't.'

'Look at me, Debbie.' I lift my arms and flex my muscles. 'I'm strong. I'll protect you, like I said I would.'

She laughs and her face softens. 'You're still just a boy.' She shakes her head. Her eyes and her cheeks are shining with tears, but she is laughing so I know everything will be all right.

I lift my fist to the sky. 'I'm strong. I will protect you.'

She laughs harder, hysterical from the pain and the anger and maybe the relief of not being alone anymore. And maybe my promise. Maybe she is laughing at my promise.

I rise to my feet and hold out my hands. 'Come

on, Debbie. Get up. Spar with me.'

She throws a punch and I duck. I jab at her, missing on purpose. She laughs and throws another punch, and another. I duck and I dodge and I block, and I throw some back, stopping short of hitting her every time. Her hair bounces as she jumps around in front of me. Light and shadows play on her face.

The tears on her face dry. Her eyes lose their soreness, her cheeks flush with excitement and she becomes as close to happy as she ever gets. Her eyes aren't happy. Her eyes are never happy, but they aren't hard anymore, they aren't angry. They are tender, and feeling, and alive.

We walk back through the woods in the last of the light. I reach out and hold her hand, like we used to do when we were little. It is soft and warm and she squeezes my hand back.

'Don't leave me with him, Debbie.' I try and look into her eyes but she turns the other way. She wraps her arm around my waist and starts humming like Mum used to.

'We'll leave together, won't we?' My voice sounds uncertain. I hate myself for it.

Wind rustles the leaves, sweeps between the trees and billows our tops, and we walk home, back to the block of flats, where the window is on the eighth floor and there is no escape.

CHAPTER TEN

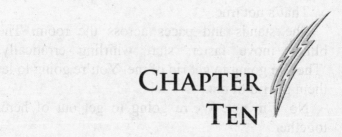

The blinds are swaying in a breeze; the air is cool and fresh. I wonder if a window is open. I get up and look but there is no window you can open.

I feel a pain in my chest and I see her. She's in a corner, all small and tight, knees up to her chest. I hate it when she is like this. I don't know what to do.

Debbie?

'Leave me alone.'

I sit next to her. I reach out to her, but I still can't do it, I can't touch her. I lower my arm and stare at the blinds swaying.

Please, Debbie.

'Please what?'

Stop it.

She lifts her head and glares at me. 'Why? Why

should I stop? To make you feel better?'

No, I want you to feel better.

'No you don't. You don't care about me, you never did.'

That's not true.

She stands and paces across the room. The blinds move faster, start whirling erratically. 'They're going to get rid of me. You're going to let them get rid of me.'

No, I'm not. We're going to get out of here, together.

I stand and block her path, to try and stop her pacing, to try and make her look at me, to make her see I am telling the truth.

She starts jumping around in front of me, punching the air near my face. 'Spar with me Paul.' Her eyes are red and puffy.

No.

The blinds flow into the room, higher and higher, like a great wind is coming from the window, building in strength. Debbie bounces around me. 'You can't stop them. You are weak. You are a coward.' Her punches get closer. 'You couldn't stop him either, could you? All that training, all that strength, and you couldn't stop him.' My eyes sting. I tense my muscles and stand firm. 'You wouldn't stop him. You said you were going to protect me. You're a liar. A liar and a coward.' She punches me on the jaw and it hurts. It really hurts.

I look at her, but I don't know what to say. I never know what to say when she's like this.

'That's because you're stupid. It's because you don't understand. You never understood. You just let him.'

I tried, Debbie, I was going to –

'*BUT YOU DIDN'T.*' She hits me again. 'You *LISTENED* and you *WATCHED*, and you *KNEW* what was going on but you *DID NOTHING*.' She hits me again. The stitches above my eye split, and blood flows down my cheek. 'You got bigger and stronger and still you did nothing.' She hits me again and again. 'You could have stopped him, but you didn't. You're as bad as him. Worse. Because you knew it was wrong but you did *NOTHING*. You let it happen. You're a *COWARD*.'

She hits me on the chin, and on the temple, and the blinds whirl and whip around the room, and she hits me and I let her. She should hit me; she has every right to hit me. I will let her, and I won't hit back, not this time.

'Fight me, Paul.'

No.

She crumples to the floor. 'Why didn't you stop him?'

I sit on the bed and blink fast.

I wanted to, Debbie. I'm sorry.

'They're going to get rid of me, and you're going to let them.'

No, I'm not. You're staying with me. This time

I will protect you. This time I will get it right. I promise.

Oh happy day.

Please. Sing a different song.
   'I like this song.'
   She sings louder.

OH HAPPY DAY.

I turn to her and she is floating, eyes glazed, like in the pit.

When he washed

Please, Debbie. Please stop.

WHEN HE WASHED

The blinds break free of the window and hurtle across the room. The bed shakes. A storm is filling the room, and it makes no sense. It never makes sense. Is this in my head? Is this real? Debbie's voice rings out over the wind, and it doesn't make sense.

WHEN HE WASHED MY SINS AWAY.

'DEBBIE!' I shout, I can't help it. I am scared.

She turns to me, eyes angry. 'Don't let them get rid of me, Paul.'

The door opens; the wind catches it and slams it back against the wall. Three buffalo wade in, arms shielding themselves from the storm. I run at them, and I don't know if it's me pushing past them or the wind rushing around me, but they fall to the floor and they stay down.

I run into the corridor, fly past the ward window and out of the corner of my eye I see Crazy Horse, standing side by side with the Native American chief, and it occurs to me that I've completely lost my mind. The thought scares me even more and I run faster.

I run along the corridor, around a corner. Ahead of me are the doors with the stairs behind. I hurtle into them, but they don't give.

'*DEBBIE!* Help me!' I shout over the noise of the wind.

The doors shake, the lock creaks. I push with all my strength and the wind roars around me, smashes into the doors, and I feel them giving. They're going to open and we're going to get out of here.

I hear shouts. Buffalo are coming.

The wind surges and I push harder.

I feel their footsteps pounding.

Debbie!

A buffalo lands on me and I try to stand firm, but he is pulling me to the floor. Another one

lands, and another, and I am slammed into the
floor, buried by buffalo.

DEBBIE! Get them off me!

The wind blasts around us; there is a hurricane
in the corridor and the buffalo are shouting. I feel a
needle stab into my arm, the wind dies down and
my muscles give up, and everything is soft, and I
am so angry at the darkness falling over me but I
can't fight it.

CHAPTER ELEVEN

I wake on the table.

Debbie?

She doesn't answer but I know she's here, I can feel her presence.

Dr Stuart is clipping wires to my head. I stare at her but she doesn't look back.

A door swings open, light footsteps approach, and a chair is pulled up close. Dr Epstein. 'Projection was confirmed?'

'Yes.'

'How did it manifest?'

'Air flow, up to storm force. Also focused, direct force – it did this.' Dr Stuart waves her hand over my face.

Dr Epstein leans over, peers at my face, and gives me a sympathetic smile. 'I see your sister hurt you today, Paul. Don't worry; we're going to help.'

'I don't want you to get rid of her.'

'We don't want to get rid of your sister either, Paul.' Dr Epstein smiles. 'We simply want to help you gain control.'

'Control?'

'I understand this must be very difficult for you, but it is for the best. You'll see.' His face disappears from view as he sits down. 'Activity?'

'38%.'

'Has prep 1 been administered?'

'Yes.'

'Hmmm.' He sounds disappointed.

'He was heavily sedated on arrival.'

'I see. Proceed with prep 2.'

A buffalo injects cold. I hear Debbie humming. Debbie?

'Don't let them get rid of me.'

'88%.'

'Proceed with H.'

They inject black into my veins and the darkness of space envelopes me, lifts me into the belly of the universe. Stars appear, one by one, until they surround me, above, below. I look down. Something else is below me, far away.

'1%.'

'Excellent.'

'Holding steady.'

I swim down. I know something is down there. I

swim through space until I hit water, black warm water, filled with stars. I hold my breath and I swim deeper and deeper. I know something is down here.

'1.2%.'

I see a body, floating far below. I swim faster. It's a girl. I know her; she looks a little like me. I reach her, I grab her, I pull her and I swim up; I pull her up and we breach the surface and I hold her tight and I breathe. She's not moving, not breathing. I hold her and I keep swimming. She is heavy. I wish she would wake up.

'1.5%.'

My feet hit mud and I stand. I drag her from the water and lay her down on the mud and I pump on her chest and I breathe into her lungs.

'2%.'

She coughs out water, she looks at me, and I know who she is. This time I'll save her. She is staying with me.

'7%.'

She looks at me and she stands and she swims up through space and I follow her.

'50%.'

'Repeat H.'

Blackness hits me but I push it away.

'Still rising.'

I open my eyes. I know where I am.

'100%.'

'Repeat H.'

I hear Debbie singing.

I TAUGHT HIM TO FIGHT AND I TAUGHT HIM TO FIGHT AND I TAUGHT HIM TO FIGHT

'Still rising.'

Wind rushes around me. The table shakes. The restraints loosen.

'200%.' I hear panic in Dr Stuart's voice. I think I smell her fear.

'Administer F.'

'F.'

Rocks fall. I smash them away. The whole room is shaking. Dr Epstein is out of his seat, shouting at Dr Stuart.

'Double dose, G and H.'

Dr Stuart isn't responding. I turn to her. My head can turn. The restraints are loose.

Her nose is bleeding; she is staring at the ceiling.

I look up and I see Debbie. She is floating above us, looking right at Dr Stuart and singing.

I taught him to fight and I taught him to pray
Oh happy day.

Dr Epstein is scrambling around. He grabs a handful of syringes and moves to my arm.

I fight, I fight so hard, and the table is shaking,

and the restraints are loosening, but there are buffalo everywhere holding me down and I feel the blackness injected into my hand, and the universe into my neck, and more blackness in my arm, and more stars, and more water, and more rocks, and the bed stops shaking and I can't hear Debbie anymore. I am drifting away into the loneliness of space...

'Dr Stuart? DR STUART.'

'Yes?'

'Activity?'

'2%.'

She is far away. They are all far away.

'Heavy sedation.'

They inject warm, and I want to be angry but I don't have the energy.

'Schedule surgery for intracranial monitors as soon as possible.'

I need to fight, but I don't have the energy. I don't even have the energy to keep my eyelids from shutting.

CHAPTER TWELVE

I am doing press ups in my room, in the flat on the eighth floor, where the window doesn't lead to the safety of the woods. My heart is pounding and sweat drips from my forehead. I hear the door. Not my door. Debbie's door.

Without thinking, I run. I crash through doors and run at him and he turns and I throw a punch. It smashes into his jaw and he reels back and I keep attacking, bearing down on him as he staggers back. A left hook, a right uppercut, a right hook connects with the side of his head and he falls to the floor and he swipes with his legs and I fall down and then he is on me and he is mad.

His fists fly into my head, the left side, the right side, my jaw, my temple, and my whole head is growing, throbbing, pounding, breaking. I can't move but I am vaguely aware that my body is shaking and drool or blood is spilling from my mouth. I try to squeeze my eyes shut but even they don't work. I just see his fists, flying towards me and black and red and flashes of light and dark.

Something is hissing. It might be me, trying to breathe, air escaping from my lungs. There is a high pitched scream, going on and on and on. I think it might be Debbie.

A siren is wailing above my head. People are drifting in and out of focus. Green uniforms. Determined, focused, caring eyes. Paramedics. Debbie is with me. Her voice moves the air. She is talking about boxing. Covering his tracks.

My head is smashed open. I can feel the blood pulsing out of it, seeping into the sheets beneath me, warm and wet. I feel it trickling down my chin and pooling on my neck. This is it. The end of me, and I didn't protect her. I wasn't strong enough. I was never strong enough.

CHAPTER THIRTEEN

My mouth is dry. I know something is wrong as soon as I wake. I can't feel Debbie; I can't feel her at all. Someone shines a light into one of my eyes, then the other. It pierces like a needle and I wince at the pain. My head aches. It aches so much, and it is sore, and cold and numb, all at the same time.

'Paul?'

I know that voice. I open my eyes and everything is light, but it's a softer light than on the table, and I can't move, but there are no restraints. It's just that I am too heavy, and I don't want to; I don't want to in case I fall apart.

'Paul?'

I know that voice. I hate that voice.

'Do you remember me, Paul? It's Dr Epstein.'

I stare at him, hard. I want to punch the

sympathetic smile from his face.

'How are you feeling?'

Anger wells inside me, suffocates me. I want to say that when I am strong I will show him how it feels, I will show him how it feels to have someone smash your head open and wrap it in bandages and then ask how it feels, but all that comes out of my mouth is a burbling groan.

'Can you move your fingers?'

I try to clench my fists. My fingers are slow, weak.

'I have good news for you, Paul. We have established which medications can be used to control your condition.' He looks at me like he expects me to smile back. 'To ensure they are working effectively we have inserted a couple of intracranial monitors.' His eyes drift to the top of my head. 'They will monitor your brain and alert us if any abnormal activity occurs, so we can address it as soon as possible.'

I lift my hand to my head.

'Don't touch your head, Paul.' He raises his hand like he's going to brush mine away, but he doesn't. 'The procedure to insert the monitors was minimally invasive, but it will take at least a week for the skin to heal.'

I feel sick.

'Over the next few days you may experience some headaches, confusion, dizziness, perhaps some nausea, and you will feel a little weak,' he flashes his sympathetic smile again, 'but this is normal. You'll feel better soon, and then we'll move you to a ward. Once we're sure the medications are working effectively, we plan to transfer you to Tŷ Eidolon. You can start a new life there.'

I don't know where or what Tŷ Eidolon is, but it doesn't matter. Before they send me anywhere else I am going to escape. I am going to find Debbie, and I am going to get us out of here.

'For now, you need to rest.' He nods to a buffalo hovering just behind me, and before I can move my hand away I am injected with sleep.

I am swimming in black water, looking for Debbie. But as soon as I see her they come and inject me and she drifts away. It happens over and over, again and again, until I feel hope draining away, despair and loneliness closing around me like a thick, black fog.

Seconds pass in hours and days pass in seconds. Time is inconsistent, confusing, an undefined blur. When buffalo bring food I eat it. When they drag me to the toilet I think about fighting and running, but my body is heavy and limp and the floor slopes and tilts and I slide back to this bed. I always end up back on this bed, looking for Debbie in the darkest parts of my mind. And when I find her, they come and inject me and she drifts away.

At first I have fleeting moments with her, just a glimpse of her floating hair or her glazed eyes. But as time goes on it takes the buffalo longer to come, and the moments become minutes. Sometimes I hear her singing, sometimes I see her sat on the window ledge strumming the blinds.

The buffalo change my dressings and I let them. I will heal, and get stronger, and I will find Debbie and get us out of here. I have to stay angry. When they inject me I float, and swim, and sink, and drift, but all the time I stay angry. I hold on to my anger because that's what keeps me sane and makes me strong. I have to stay angry so I can get out of here, so I can find Debbie and we can get out of here, together.

A buffalo arrives and I want to be angry, but it's Pam. She knew Debbie, and that makes me as close to Debbie as I have been in days, and right now that just makes me feel so empty and alone that my eyes sting and I have to blink to stop the tears from flowing.

'It's not that bad,' Pam unravels my dressing, 'although they have messed your hair up again.' She sucks in air through pursed lips. 'And after I went to the trouble of tidying it up.' The air hits my scalp and it feels raw. Pam wraps a fresh bandage around my head. 'You're scheduled to go to a ward tomorrow. Things are looking up for you. The good Lord has a plan.' For a second she looks like she wants to smile, but then she just shakes her head and walks away and I am left alone. No breeze, no wind. No Debbie.

CHAPTER
FOURTEEN

Debbie is singing in front of the choir. She leads them all, singing joyfully. She is the smallest, the youngest, but she has the biggest voice. The illusion of great happiness plays across her face. But I know better. I know that make-up covers bruises and streaks made by years of tears. I know her smile dresses anger, her shining eyes blind the pain.

Suddenly she is gone and the choir is solemn. Some of the women are crying, tears rolling down their fat cheeks. I see Pam in the middle of them. Her face is hard, her fists clenched. I look at Debbie's coffin and my breath catches in my throat, choking me, suffocating me. I am weak. I'm a coward. I failed her. I killed her.

The wind is blowing through the trees around

the graveyard. It sweeps between the gravestones and billows the robes of the choir gathered around the grave. Her coffin is lowered into the ground. The priest is talking but I don't hear his words.

People file away until no one is left but me and the policeman by my side. And the gravediggers, standing off to the side. I see a shovel pushed into the ground; I walk to it and grab it and start shovelling the earth over her coffin, my eyes stinging in the wind. The policeman doesn't stop me. The gravediggers don't stop me. They let me bury her. I fill the hole with earth and snot and tears. Then I fall to my knees in the dirt. The policeman pulls me up and leads me away.

CHAPTER FIFTEEN

I wake somewhere new. The light is different, the bed is different, and there is a small child in front of me, staring at me intently.

'I'm Saeed. What's your name?' He is bald with fresh scars on his head and wires coming out from behind his ears, and he is wearing a yellow overall like mine, except his is like a tent on his small and skinny frame. 'Do you hear things?'

I listen for Debbie. She's not here.

'I hear things. Do you hear things?'

'I guess so.' My voice is croaky; like I haven't used it in a long time.

'I hear my grandmother.' Saeed leans close and looks from side to side, as if someone unseen might be eavesdropping. 'She's dead,' he whispers, then he leans back and asks louder, 'What's your name?'

'Paul.' I look around the room. There is a large table in the middle, bolted down. No chairs. A bed is in each corner. Curtains are drawn around one of the beds near the window.

'That's Ricardo's bed. Ric hears things too. He says they are spirits. He's nice, he laughs a lot.' Saeed looks at the bandages around my head. 'They put wires in your head, too?'

I nod. It generates a wave of dizziness and makes my head ache.

'Did they hear what you hear?'

'What?' I don't understand.

'They heard my grandmother,' Saeed whispers. 'That's why they put the wires in my head. Did they hear what you hear?'

'I don't know.' Did they hear Debbie? I try to remember the events that led up to this moment, but everything is a blur and I'm not sure what is real and what is not any more.

I look at the bed opposite Ric's. It's empty, but the sheets are crumpled.

'That's my bed, and the other one,' Saeed points to the empty bed opposite mine, 'is Tom's, but he's not here. They took him away and I don't think he's coming back. Does your head hurt?'

'A little.'

'Mine too. It's getting better, though. Dr Stuart says it will help them find the right medications to control my condition.' He sounds like he is reciting a line he has heard a thousand times before. He leans close to me again and speaks so softly I can barely hear him. 'I hope they stop her. She scares me. She groans and wails in the night. Do your voices scare you?'

I shake my head slightly; try to move it without causing another wave of dizziness. Debbie doesn't scare me. Not often.

'What do you hear?' Saeed asks.

His eyes are round, huge in his face. He looks so young, so fragile. 'How old are you?' I ask, not wanting to talk about Debbie.

'Ten.' Saeed straightens his back. 'My grandmother says I'm a late developer. I'll be big and strong one day, like you and Ric.' He looks at the curtains around Ric's bed. 'Ric isn't scared of anything. I'll be like that when I'm big.'

I used to think that when I was ten; that being big and strong would take the fear away. It doesn't. I close my eyes to try and stop the spinning.

'You're tired, aren't you?'

'I guess so.'

'Ric says your spirit brings the wind. That you will free us.'

I hear what he says but I don't try to make sense of it. My eyes are closing and I can see Debbie; she is far away but I can see her, and I know I am going to reach her. I am going to reach her soon. When the buffalo come with their needles I don't care because I know I am going to reach her soon, and there is nothing they can do about it.

CHAPTER
SIXTEEN

I feel sunshine, warm on my face, and hear a child laughing. For a moment I don't know where I am, but then I see the blinds, like bars on a cage. The sun is high in the sky behind them and silhouetted in front of the window Saeed is being thrown around by Crazy Horse, and he is laughing uncontrollably. One second he's upside down, the next the right way up, then Crazy Horse is spinning him over his head and I think he's going to drop him, he's going to drop the little boy and he'll break, but Saeed just keeps on laughing. I feel something, like a twinge of happiness reaching out from Saeed and infecting me, and it hurts because it's just an illusion. There is no joy or happiness in this place. I have to stay angry.

Crazy Horse sees me and throws Saeed onto his

bed. He bounces off and hits the floor but he's still laughing, laughing so much he can't breathe properly and he just lies there trying to catch his breath. Crazy Horse rushes towards me, jumps and lands on the foot of my bed cross-legged, and the shock jars my whole body and makes my head ache more, and I think the bed is going to collapse but it doesn't.

'Pablo,' he beams, his eyes shining with so much excitement it just doesn't seem right.

'Paul,' I croak.

'Pablo,' he nods. His yellow overall is half undone, the arms tied around his waist, and he is covered in tattoos, symbols made of simple shapes and lines. Circles, squares and triangles overlap to create angular birds, snakes, mountains, and other things I couldn't guess at. Some of the tattoos are professionally done, but most are homemade scrawls with no thought to order or beauty.

Crazy Horse points to one on his arm. The outline of a man, drawn simply with straight lines, stands inside a diamond. 'That's you,' he says. 'Chief Crazy Horse gave me a vision of you. Your spirit brings the wind and you will save her.' He blows out slowly and his arms float away from him, then he jumps off my bed, and runs towards Saeed yelling, picks him up, and throws him around again.

Dr Stuart comes into the room, three buffalo behind her.

'How are you feeling, Paul?'

I don't answer.

'Someone will bring you food shortly. We have decided to start you on oral medication. If you take your pills without complaint, there will be less need for the injections. How does that sound?' She raises her eyebrows but still manages to look stern.

Perhaps I can pretend to take the pills, spit them out. Even if I can't, I will still find Debbie.

Dr Stuart moves to Saeed's bed. Crazy Horse is on the other side of it, holding Saeed by his ankles, upside down behind his back.

'Put him down, Ricardo.'

Ric doesn't move. He just stands there, smiling at Dr Stuart, Saeed giggling behind his back.

'Ricardo, I've talked to you about this. Saeed has had a serious operation. You are putting him at risk with all this ...' She gives up talking to Ric and nods to a buffalo. 'I need to examine Saeed.'

A buffalo approaches Ric and he adjusts Saeed so he is holding both legs with one hand, and he raises his other hand, fist clenched, towards the buffalo.

'Fight me for him,' Ric smiles, like it's all a game. 'I'll beat you one handed.'

Saeed is laughing, hitting Ric on the back. 'It's all right, Ric,' he says, 'let her look at me.'

Ric swings Saeed round and drops him onto the bed. He wanders off to his corner of the room and Dr Stuart inspects Saeed's head.

Another buffalo enters with food and a small pot of pills for me. I look at them, and then at the buffalo. Dr Stuart glances over to me. 'There are painkillers, antibiotics to stop your head getting infected and your medication.'

I stare at the pills. They want me to take them voluntarily. They want me to knowingly push Debbie away.

'If you don't take them, we'll inject.'

I breathe in deeply and take the pills. I'll take them today, but soon I'll be strong enough. I won't stay here much longer; I will get out, and no matter how many pills they give me, I will find Debbie before I go.

The buffalo leaves, and returns with food and pills for Ric. They stare at each other until the buffalo glances away to the window and Ric grabs the food, sits on his bed, and eats.

'Your pills, Ricardo,' Dr Stuart looks up from Saeed. The buffalo near her walks towards Ric.

Ric carries on eating.

'Your pills, Ricardo,' Dr Stuart says again.

Ric stands up, looks at the four buffalo that now surround him, and chants loudly, hopping from one foot to the other and swinging his arms back and forth. He grabs the pot of pills from the buffalo, downs them, throws the pot on the floor, opens his mouth wide and looks round at the buffalo, sticking his tongue out and hissing. They back away, content he has taken the pills.

Dr Stuart injects Saeed with something, and his eyes close. She walks to the door without saying anything else, and the buffalo file out after her.

Ric sits on his bed with his back to me, looking out of the window. Every so often he laughs or says something in a language I don't understand. I eat slowly, trying not to move my head too much. By the time I've finished Ric isn't talking to his voices anymore. He's not smiling, and it makes him look completely different; tense and serious.

'They have taken my spirits away.' He stands and paces the room.

I wonder if he misses his voices like I miss Debbie.

Ric stops abruptly, turns to the window, and his smile, his enormous manic smile, spreads across his face again, and for some reason it makes me feel better. 'But they will return,' he beams. He bounces over and sits on the end of my bed. 'They try to control the spirits,' he looks to the door and whispers, 'they want to use them for their own gain.'

Ric looks crazy. Sounds crazy. But then what am I? Do I sound as crazy as him?

'They have to be stopped.' His eyes are shining, excited. 'Some people,' he says, 'have spirits so powerful they can't be controlled. That's what will stop them.'

I am lost for words. Ric makes no sense at all.

'Angharad,' Ric smiles. 'She's one of them.'

'One of who?'

'You will save her and she will stop them.' He points to a tattoo on his arm, near the diamond symbol he showed me earlier. There is a jagged line with an arrow head, something like a symbol for lightning, plunging into a ring of concentric circles, circles within circles like a target, that look fractured, smashed. 'You will free her, and she will stop them.'

'Stop who?'

Ric rolls his eyes at me. 'Those that try to control the spirits.'

'The doctors?'

Ric nods, 'And who they work for.'

'Who do they work for?'

Ric points to the tattoo of the concentric circles again.

The door opens, and I'm relieved; I don't understand Ric at all. A couple of buffalo step into the room. They clear away the food trays and leave a handful of battered paperback books on the table. Ric takes one to his corner of the room and pulls the curtain around his bed. I hear him chanting softly behind it.

I choose a book with a huge fist on the cover, but when I try to read it I see Debbie floating in the distance. I call to her, but she doesn't hear me. I close my eyes and try to follow her. I can't lose her. I have to reach her, and get us out of here.

I am lying on sand, water lapping at my feet. I have been washed up by the black ocean but Debbie is still out there, lost at sea. I will get up and swim to her. I try and move but I am buried in the sand, and the more I struggle the more it tightens around me, and there is something in the sand, something strange that grabs my arms and sucks my strength away.

A groan reverberates through my dream. I open my eyes but it's dark. The groan is in the room. It circles the ceiling, increasing in pitch and volume until it is a wail. It's like the cry of an old woman; breathless, confused and alone. A separate scream comes from the bed next to me and I realise it's coming from Saeed.

The shadow of Ric moves to Saeed's bed. He bundles him in his arms, sits on the bed with him, and Saeed stops screaming. The wail in the room dies down to a groan, and Saeed whimpers like a hurt dog. 'Make her stop, Ric. Make her stop,' he pleads.

Ric starts singing, chanting firm and solemn. He stamps his foot on the floor to make a slow and steady beat, and he rocks Saeed back and forth.

Hey, hey, watenay
Hey, hey, watenay
Kay-o-kay-nah
Kay-o-kay-nah.

The groan fades to a whisper and Saeed is quiet.

But then the buffalo come. They storm into the room and in an instant there is chaos. One of them tries to wrestle Saeed from Ric, and he shouts, 'Leave him, he's fine. *GET OFF HIM!*'

Saeed screams and the wail fills the room again. It is deafening, and Ric is shouting and the buffalo are piling into him.

I want to fight. I want to get up and fight with Ric, but I am still trapped in the sand. I struggle against it, and eventually I get my arms free and I sit up. I swing my legs out of bed and see Saeed being taken by a buffalo, and Ric is surrounded by more.

I stand and I see Debbie, floating outside the window, and a gentle breeze flows over me. I move to the buffalo but I am too late. They are injecting Saeed and they are injecting Ric, and Dr Stuart has appeared and she is shouting at a buffalo and he grabs me and injects me too, and the moment is gone.

CHAPTER SEVENTEEN

A door bursts open. Not my door. Debbie's. In the flat on the eighth floor, where there is no escape through the window.

My father shouts a slur of garbled words, in the way he does when he is drunk. Debbie responds, in the way she does when she is scared but doesn't want to show it. I stand and stare at my door. I am going to open it. I am going to open it and charge into Debbie's room and knock him down.

There is a scuffle and a thud. Then the crying starts. The pleading. Fear seeps through the wall between us. I stare at the handle on the door until my eyes burn. Why can't I move?

Banging. Screaming. Shouting. A whimper, a sob. Something heavy falls over and smashes. I stare at the door, tears streaming down my face.

Hate wells up like bile in my throat. Why can't I move?

I think of the trophy, the brass boxing glove hidden under my bed. Three years in a row. Under fourteen champion. But I can't protect my sister. I'm not even trying. I can't move. Why can't I move?

I stare at the door. Three feet and a million miles away. The handle within my reach but at the end of an endless tunnel. I smell my fear, sharp and stale. It suffocates me. I can't breathe. I can't move. I can't think. I moan, loud enough to block out the noise but quiet enough that he doesn't hear me. I hate myself. I'm a coward. Weak. Useless. Ashamed.

A gentle breeze flows from the open window behind me, the eighth floor window, where there is no escape, and I miss the bungalow, and the woods behind it.

CHAPTER EIGHTEEN

Air bursts into my lungs. I feel heavy and weak, and I look at the blinds and I'm angry with myself for being so weak. I need to get stronger, and I need to get out of here. I sit up and my head spins. I hear a deep, throaty laugh. Ric is sitting on his bed, his back to me, muttering away in a foreign language. Saeed is not here.

I stand, and stretch, and breathe. I look at the trees through the gaps in the blinds; stare at a single point, waiting for the dizziness to stop. I need to get stronger. I need to get out of here. I lower myself slowly to the floor and start doing press ups. One. Two. My muscles are weak, my head heavy. I hear Ric move towards me, still muttering to himself, and I feel his foot press gently onto my back.

'Get off me.' I turn my head and stare at him.

He laughs and presses harder, crushing my chest into the floor until I can't breathe. 'You're weak,' he says.

I push up with all my strength, get on to my knees, and Ric steps off me. I stand and look him in the eye.

His face lights up. 'You are weak and you are a coward.'

His words hit me hard: they are Debbie's words. Anger surges through me and I clench my fists. He is not allowed to steal Debbie's words.

'They took Saeed. They came and took Saeed and you could have stopped them but you did nothing.' He is still smiling at me, like this is all a game, and I want to punch the smile from his face.

The door opens and two buffalo walk into the room. One of them is Pam. She looks at Ric all stern but he just smiles at her, glides towards her, takes her hand – the one not holding the pot of pills – and starts dancing with her. I sit down on my bed, the room spinning again.

'You're dancing well today, Ric,' Pam laughs and sways her enormous hips. They dance over to Ric's corner of the room and the other buffalo passes me a pot of pills. I take them from him, and stare at them. He stares at me. I turn away and look at Ric. He is sitting on his bed now, holding Pam's fingers and looking up at her with pleading eyes. Pam pulls her hand away, glances at the other buffalo, then palms Ric's pills and passes him the empty pot. She slips the pills in her pocket, leans towards Ric and whispers something, then walks over to me.

'So you've made it to a ward,' she unwraps the bandage around my head.

'Where's Saeed?' I ask.

'With Dr Stuart. He should be back this afternoon.'

'There was a noise last night –'

'I know,' Pam cuts me short, 'Saeed screams a great deal when he is distressed. Don't let it concern you, he is in good hands.' The bandage falls away and my head feels cold. I stare at the pills in my hand. 'Are you going to take them?' Pam asks.

I turn and look her in the eye, 'I saw ...' I glance over to Ric. She didn't make him take his pills.

'Shush now,' she says firmly. She looks up to the other buffalo. He has wandered to the window, is staring through the blinds. 'What you see and what you understand are two different things.' She inspects the scars on my head, 'Are you going to take them?' she asks again.

'They push Debbie away.'

Pam nods. 'Yes, they will.' She has gone hard. 'I am going to leave your dressing off. It's healing fine.'

'Please,' I try again.

'Look Paul,' she sighs, 'you and Ric are very

95

different.' She leans forwards and whispers into my ear, 'I've known Ric a long time, and I know sometimes he is happier with his voices than without. Not always, but sometimes.' She moves around and looks me in the eye, 'I don't know you as well as I know Ric, but I do know you have to move on. Debbie is gone, and you can't move forwards until you leave her behind. Now, are you going to take those pills or am I going to call him over?' She nods to the buffalo.

I hesitate, but I take the pills. I'll take them today, but tomorrow...

'All done,' Pam announces and she moves to the door. She glances back at Ric and gives him a stern look. 'Don't go filling Paul's head with your nonsense. He needs to rest.'

Another buffalo appears and puts two trays of food on the table, and they all leave. I take my tray to my bed. Ric sits on the table in front of me and eats, staring at my head. Every so often he mumbles something or laughs. My head is cold, and the scars are itching. I want to know what they have done, but I can't bring myself to touch it.

'Ric?' I ask, 'How many wires do I have in my head?'

'One either side. Like antennae.'

Ric's hair is long and straight and black. 'You don't have any wires?'

'They haven't seen me project.' He beams, clearly proud of himself.

'Project?'

'That's what they call it when other people hear your voices, or see your spirits, or if your spirits can do things,' his eyes light up, 'like bring the wind.'

I remember running down the corridor, the wind rushing around me. But that wasn't real. Was it? How does Ric know these things?

'If you project your spirits out, if they see you, they put wires in,' Ric looks up at my head, 'to study them, to try and control them.'

'So you don't have wires because you don't project?'

'I didn't say that,' Ric smiles. 'I said they haven't seen me project.' He glances to the corridor window and I look up just in time to see a feather headdress disappear out of sight. 'I just know how to keep my spirits to myself.'

'How –'

'Many spirits talk to me,' Ric interrupts, 'Great chiefs, warriors, hunters, Shamans, medicine men.' He looks straight into my eyes. 'Debbie.'

I feel anger welling up. Debbie is mine; he has no right to talk to her.

Ric bursts into song.

Oh happy day.

'Don't sing that,' I shout over him. He has no right to sing her song.

'Why not?' Ric stands.

I stare at him, anger rising, burning. I stand too.

'She has a nice voice. How did she die?'

My heart freezes, my hands feel hot.

'How did she die?'

I sit, turn away from him.

'Fine. Debbie will tell me.'

My fists burn, anger overwhelms me. I stand again and I shout, '*DEBBIE ISN'T HERE.*'

Ric steps forward. 'She is in the spirit world,' he presses his finger hard into my temple, 'and she is in here.'

'If she's in *MY* head then how do *YOU* hear her?' I am so confused. Am I crazy, or is Ric crazy, or are we both crazy?

'You *PROJECT* her out,' he says, 'like Saeed does with his grandmother, and Angharad does with her sisters, and Tyrone, and Davis, and plenty of others who have come here but aren't here anymore.' Ric stops smiling. 'They study you, they test drugs on you, they find ways to control your spirits. If you look like you might be useful to them they send you to Tŷ Eidolon, and if you don't they pull you to pieces. Dissect you.'

That can't be true. I feel sick. 'But the families…?'

'No one here has a family,' he says. 'We are all lost, unknown, forgotten …' His voice trails away and he chants something unintelligible with no tune. He moves to his corner of the room, sits on his bed with his back to me, and mumbles to his voices.

I lean back against the wall. I feel sick. I have to get out of here. This place is all kinds of wrong. Whether Ric is telling the truth or not, whatever goes on in here, I don't want to know. I just want to leave. I just want to find Debbie and get out of here. I am almost pleased when the black water washes over me, sending me into darkness. The stars are a comfort, and I feel Debbie. She is somewhere in the distance. I will find her and we will get out of here, together.

I am vaguely aware of buffalo bringing more food, but I am floating on water, listening for Debbie. I think Ric is shouting at them, throwing punches. There is a scuffling and a thud and I think maybe I should get up, but I want to stay here and look for Debbie.

When I wake, Ric is standing over me, bouncing around, fists raised. 'They came and you did nothing. You are weak and you are a coward.' He throws a punch towards my face.

I grab his arm and grip it tight and I pull myself out of bed and I shout at him, '*DON'T HIT ME!*'

He laughs and he throws another punch.

I let go of him, duck, and raise my fists. A breeze hits my face. The blinds flow into the room and Ric laughs louder. He hits me, on the chin, and again, on the cheek. He is fast. He is fast and I am slow. I clench my fists and I watch him.

'You are weak and you are a coward. You're as bad as them, worse, because you know what they're doing is wrong, but you do nothing. You let it happen.'

He is stealing Debbie's words again. I won't let him. I throw a punch, but Ric dodges it. He throws one back and it smashes into my jaw.

The wind picks up. I feel a storm coming. I put all my weight into a punch and it lands on Ric's jaw; he staggers back and slips, and the wind pins him down and he is laughing, laughing so hard, and his eyes are shining with excitement.

'You bring the wind!' Ric shouts as he struggles to his feet. The wind is whipping his hair around his face, and he is smiling and laughing and shouting, and shaking his arms in triumph.

I look to the window and I see Debbie, floating outside, and my heart beats faster and my anger ebbs away.

The door opens and I am about to turn and throw myself at the buffalo when I see he is carrying Saeed, and he looks so small and frail and broken it stops me in my tracks, and the wind stops, and Debbie is gone.

CHAPTER NINETEEN

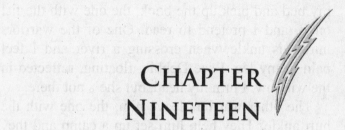

Saeed is pale, sweating and trembling.

'What did they do?' Ric sits next to him.

'They tried a new medicine. Because my grandmother came last night.' Saeed looks across at me. 'Did she scare you?'

I shake my head.

'The noises she makes …' Saeed's voice wavers. 'I don't know what she wants.'

Ric puts his hand on Saeed's forehead. 'You're hot.'

Saeed nods, 'Dr Stuart said to rest and I'll feel better soon.'

Ric looks out of the window and mutters something foreign.

'Tell me a story, Ric.' Saeed puts his hand over Ric's and it makes Ric jump, but then he shuffles back onto the bed, crosses his legs and smiles.

'Which one?'

'The one about the skeleton.'

Ric starts to tell a story about a group of warriors who go hunting in the mountains. I go to my bed and pick up the book, the one with the fist on it, and I pretend to read. One of the warriors hurts his ankle when crossing a river and I feel pain in my leg. I see Debbie, floating, reflected in the window. I turn my head, but she's not there.

The other warriors leave him, the one with the hurt ankle. They help him set up a camp and they go into the mountains without him. I glimpse a campfire in my peripheral vision in the corner of the room, but when I turn my head there's nothing there.

The warrior is alone for days. His ankle doesn't get better; it's swollen and painful. He runs out of food, and a snowstorm traps him in his camp. The room gets colder and I hear snow crunching, compacting under hooves. A deer wanders into the camp, rooting for grass under the snow. I can hear its breathing, feel its warmth. All of a sudden I notice a warrior, a Native American warrior, crouched on Ric's bed, bow and arrow raised. He looks as real as me, as real as Debbie. My breath catches in my throat as he takes aim. The bow string is taught, his eyes focused on me. The arrow flies and disappears somewhere between us but I hear the deer fall, see its last breath make a warm cloud into the icy air.

We are all in a tent; I'm not sure when the cracked green walls became soft animal hide, when our hard metal beds became mounds of animal fur. Darkness falls quickly, and I can no longer see the tent lining, although I can hear it beating softly in the breeze. I smell meat cooking. Footsteps approach.

Debbie?

It's not Debbie. I reach for the bow and arrow at my side. The footsteps get closer. I pull the arrow back, aim into the darkness behind the fire.

A tall, thin figure in a long robe steps forward into the orange light. Its head is hung low, its face lost inside a cavernous hood. The flames flicker and shadows play across the dark folds of the robe and I feel cold. The arrow trembles.

'Don't be frightened,' a hoarse voice crackles across the fire.

I stare at the hood, follow the robe down to the floor, and see skeleton feet beneath it, sinking into snow. 'I helped you. Now it's your turn to help me.' A sleeve rises over the fire; skeleton fingers extend from it and spread out. 'I am hungry.'

I put some meat onto the bony hand and it rises to the hood. The head lifts, the hood falls back, and the firelight and the shadows dance over a human skull beneath. The jaw falls open and the skeleton hand puts the meat inside and I watch the skull chew and swallow and the meat disappear into the robe.

'I broke your ankle,' the skull whispers across the fire, 'so you would not go hunting in the mountains.' The bony hand lifts the hood back over the skull. 'Your friends have all been killed. If you had been with them you would have died, too.' The skeleton reaches out and touches my ankle and the pain and swelling vanish. 'I will lead you back to your village.'

All of a sudden the skeleton vanishes, the fire vanishes, and we are in a pale green room with cracked walls and hard metal beds and blinds on the window like bars. Ric stands and walks to his corner of the room and I realise Saeed is asleep.

I put the book down, the book with the fist, and I lean back against the wall.

'How do you do that?' I ask.

Ric turns to me and smiles. 'Pablo?'

'Paul.'

'I don't want to fight you. I want to fight with you, and get them out here.'

'Who?'

'Angharad. Saeed.' He smiles his manic smile. 'As many as we can.'

'How many are there?'

'Angharad, Saeed. Davis, Tyrone, Griff. Madeline.'

Six, and Ric. Seven. I can't get seven people out of here. I wouldn't know where to start. I shake my head.

'We can do it, Paul,' Ric nods and I notice he used my name. 'Chief Red Cloud sent me a vision. We will know when the time is right.'

I shake my head again. I can't get seven people, seven crazy, disturbed children, out of here with the help of one crazy horse.

'We can do it, Pablo. You are strong. And Debbie brings the wind.' Ric draws the curtain around his bed, and I hear him chanting and muttering behind it.

I can't sleep. When I close my eyes I see Debbie, floating in the pit. I call to her but she doesn't hear me. I drag her from the water but she is lifeless. No matter how much I pump on her chest and breathe into her lungs, she remains empty. I feel dizzy. When I open my eyes, the room spins. I can't breathe.

I get up and do press ups. One. Two. I have to get out of here. Three. Four. As my muscles warm up, I hear her singing.

Oh happy day
Oh happy day
Oh when he washed
He washed my sins away.

This time I will save her. I pump harder. Nine. Ten.

'Paul?' Debbie is sitting on my bed.

105

I freeze. I want to rush to her and hold her, but I freeze.

She stands and starts bouncing around. 'Spar with me, Paulie.'

I get up and jump around in front of her. She throws punches at the air in front of my face. I blink fast, but it's tears of relief that want to flow this time, not tears of pain. Debbie is back and we're going to get out of here.

'Who's going to get out of here, Paul?' she asks.

Me and you. We're going to get out of here together.

'What about the others?'

I can't get them out.

A breeze moves the blinds, distracts me, and Debbie punches me on the jaw. 'What they're doing is wrong. You know it's wrong. Are you going to do nothing?' She punches me again and I let her.

How can I get seven people out of here? And even if I did, where would we go? What would we do?

She punches me again, 'What they're doing here is *WRONG*. Are you going to do *NOTHING?*' She punches me, again and again, and the wind picks up, 'You are a *COWARD*. You are as bad as them. *WORSE*. Because you know it's wrong but you do *NOTHING*.'

The blinds flow into the room and I let her hit me. I don't know what else to do. The buffalo come and grab me and I haven't the energy to fight. I let them inject me. I push Debbie away. I float on the water and I know she is in the distance but I don't call her. I float on the water and I think and I try to make sense of it all, but I can't.

CHAPTER TWENTY

I'm woken by Ric banging the door, kicking the door, shouting in his foreign language. I sit up and I see Saeed. He is pale, white and translucent like wax, and coated in a film of sweat that glistens in the light. His lips and hands are trembling. He's sick. Really sick. I go to the door and I start banging on it, too.

My hands are aching by the time the buffalo arrive. Ric shouts at them and waves his arms, but he lets them take Saeed.

When they're gone there is a gnawing in my stomach, and it takes me a while to realise it's worry. It's been so long since I worried about someone, since there has been anyone in my life that wasn't dead. I pace the floor and I look at Ric, muttering on his bed.

I don't get any sense out of him all day. He ignores my questions, he chants and sings and talks to his voices. It seems like there is a thick, dark fog in the room and it is an effort to speak through it, walk through it. Behind it the sun rises and falls, the day drifts by, and no one comes, not even Debbie.

The light is fading when the door finally opens again and Pam walks in, carrying Saeed. He looks a little better. Relief sweeps through the room, clearing the fog, easing the tension and bringing Ric back to reality.

Pam places Saeed on his bed and smiles. 'I've arranged a bit of a treat for this evening, seeing as you're under the weather.'

Saeed's eyes light up. 'What is it?'

A couple of buffalo walk in with bean bags. They drop them on the floor between mine and Saeed's bed.

'We're getting a television night,' Saeed smiles and sits up.

More buffalo come in, carrying a huge, antiquated television set and video player. They place them on the table, facing mine and Saeed's bed. They fiddle around with buttons and wires, setting them up, then position themselves on the far side of the room.

Pam returns with a girl in yellow overalls. She has long, dark hair and a pretty face.

'Hi, Saeed.' She then smiles at me, friendly,

'Hi, I'm Madeline.'

'Paul,' I nod.

She sits on my bed, which is empty. 'Ric,' she calls, and he spins his head round, 'come and sit with me.'

Ric bounds over to her and then they are both sitting on my bed, close and whispering to each other, and Madeline is giggling. I sit next to Saeed.

Saeed looks at me, all knowing, and whispers, 'They're not really in love. Ric loves Angharad and Madeline loves Tom.'

'Tom?' I nod at the empty bed opposite mine.

'Yes.' Saeed whispers even quieter, 'Tom that is gone.'

'Where's Angharad?'

'She won't come. She can't watch television.'

'Why not?'

'When she hears voices, she makes electricity, and it breaks everything; televisions, radios, everything electrical. She even makes the lights flicker and go off.'

I guess if Debbie can bring the wind then whoever Angharad talks to can bring electricity. It's kind of comforting to know I'm not the only one.

'They put wires in her head but she fried them all and they had to take them out again.'

I wonder how I'm going to get the wires out of my head when I get out of here. I push the thought away. I look at Ric and Madeline, flirting on my bed.

'Does Madeline hear voices?' I whisper.

'She used to say saints spoke to her, told her to do things, but they found medicine that worked and she says she doesn't hear them anymore.'

'Then why is she still here?'

'I don't know.'

'How long have you been here?'

'Six months, I think,' Saeed sighs, 'and I still hear my grandmother.'

Three boys file into the room, surrounded by more buffalo. The first one is older, like me and Ric. He is tall and thin, with big, round, startled eyes. He nods to us all before sitting on a beanbag and leaning against the wall. He puts his hands behind his head and stares at the screen blankly.

'Hi, Griff,' Saeed smiles.

The two younger boys sit in front of Griff. One of them has scars all over his head, with scores of wires coming out of them. He has dark, angry eyebrows, and he stares at the screen fiercely. I feel his anger wrap around me like heat from a fire. The other boy has red hair and freckles. He looks nervous; his eyes dart around the room but settle on nothing.

The door closes and I look around. Seven patients. Five buffalo.

Pam hands out little bags of popcorn and turns the television on. An old cartoon starts and the boys on the beanbags stare at the screen. It's hard to know if they are watching it or not. Griff's face looks so blank his mind could be anywhere. The boy with the wires just looks angry and the freckled boy keeps looking away from the screen, around the room, tracking noises or movements I can't see or hear.

The cartoon finishes. Another one starts, and another.

'Do they hear voices?' I whisper to Saeed, and nod towards the boys.

Saeed points to the boy with wires. 'Tyrone hears angry voices, and when he does things bend.'

'Bend?'

'Bend and break. I guess that's why they put so many wires in his head.' Saeed points to the freckled boy. 'Davis sees shadows everywhere, and Griff,' Saeed points to the older boy, 'was in a car accident, a really bad one.'

'Does he hear voices?'

'I don't think he hears them anymore. He hardly hears real people anymore. Watch this.' Saeed throws a piece of popcorn at Griff. 'Griff? *GRIFF?*' Griff keeps staring at the screen with his big, round eyes. 'Ric says they gave him too much medicine once.'

I have to get out of here.

The cartoons go on and on, and I start to feel tired. The boys are all staring at the screen, half asleep. Ric and Madeline have stopped flirting and are lounging against the wall. Saeed has already drifted off, and I feel myself drifting too but then I hear a creak.

The television is sliding off the table, and it makes no sense until I see the table legs are bending. Before anyone reacts it picks up speed and smashes to the floor, and in an instant there are buffalo everywhere. One of them is shouting orders, and another has carried Tyrone out of the room before I even sit up. Davis, Griff and Madeline are ushered out, and then there is just Ric, Saeed and me, and a couple of buffalo clearing up the mess.

Saeed goes straight back to sleep, and Ric stumbles to his corner of the room and pulls his curtain. I hear him muttering behind it so I know he's not asleep; I know he's talking to his voices.

I go to my bed and think about the others. About getting them out of here. I don't know if any of them want to leave, or if they should. Tyrone looks angry; Saeed is sick; Davis looks nervous, scared. I don't think any of them are happy with their voices. I think they need help.

Saeed said Madeline doesn't hear voices anymore. Maybe that's what they do here; take your voices away and let you go, and maybe that's a good thing, for them, anyway. It makes sense. More sense than what Ric was saying about projecting, and controlling spirits, and dissecting people. Maybe it's not all bad here, like Pam said.

Maybe they are trying to help. Maybe the others are better off here. I can't get them out; I can't be responsible for them. I just need to get myself out. Just me and Debbie.

I am lying on the sand, washed up by the black ocean. I stand and the ground shakes. A tower rises behind me. I turn and look at it; it is a totem pole, an eagle at the top with wings outstretched.

Ric runs across the sand and throws himself onto the pole and starts climbing. Dr Epstein shouts and grabs his leg but he lifts it away and climbs higher.

'Pablo, come on,' he calls, and I find a foothold on the other side of the pole and climb up after him.

Ric is standing, balanced on the top of the pole, and I pull myself up next to him. I hear voices, but I don't know where from. I stand next to Ric and look out across the ocean and see it is full of people; Native American warriors, chiefs, women, and children.

'Look at them.' Ric sweeps his arms across the ocean surrounding us. 'My spirits. This is where I belong.' Ric reaches into his pocket and pulls out a handful of loose tobacco and he closes his eyes and chants, loud and powerful, as he sprinkles tobacco into the air. I feel wind blow across the back of my neck and I turn and see Debbie, poised on the tip of the eagle's wing.

Debbie?

'Hi, Paulie.'

What's Ric doing?

'He's making a tobacco offering. Pay attention, Paul.'

Ric chants and the voices on the ocean are a wash of noise. The thunder of hooves approaches, splashing across the water, rolling towards the shore. Ric stops chanting and stares into the distance.

'Have you heard of the white buffalo?'

I shake my head.

'A time of change is coming; Pablo, a new beginning, and she will bring it. That's why you must save her.' Ric leans towards the ocean, closer and closer, until he disappears, and I am left, balanced on the totem pole, with no Ric, and no Debbie, alone and confused.

CHAPTER TWENTY-ONE

The door heaves open. Dr Stuart and a couple of buffalo walk straight past me to Saeed. He is asleep, pale and trembling, like yesterday morning. Dr Stuart pulls the curtain around his bed and stays there for what seems like hours. I hear movement, but no words. When she draws the curtain I see Saeed lying back, eyes half closed, but awake. Dr Stuart moves to the door and I brace myself to speak to her.

'Is he all right?'

She sighs and turns to me. 'He has an infection. We'll do everything we can.' She continues to the door. 'I'll see you later today, Paul.'

Buffalo arrive with food, but no pills for me today. I think about what Dr Stuart said about seeing me later and I think about no pills, and I know they will be connected. I know I will be on that table later. Unless I can get out of here first.

I step out of bed and stretch. I need to get out of here. The door opens and I turn, ready to try, but it's Pam and she's carrying a guitar, and I hesitate. The door closes and as it shuts I glimpse a few buffalo behind it. I'm not sure how many.

Pam brings the guitar to Ric. His eyes light up and he reaches for it, but she pulls it away and offers a pot of pills with her other hand. He groans, a deep, guttural groan, and shakes his head, but he downs the pills and then Pam passes him the guitar. He tunes it as Pam leaves and I look to the door again. Four buffalo. There are four buffalo out there.

Ric beats the strings ferociously, and somehow an angry tune manages to wrestle its way out of the discordant chords blasting through the air. He groans over the noise, and slowly it turns into a song, a moaning song in his foreign language. Ric hunches over the guitar and his song fills the room, rising and falling with surges of anger and lulls of defeat.

The door opens again, and a girl walks into the room, with Pam behind her, four buffalo still hovering further back. The girl is wearing the yellow overalls of a patient and she's carrying another guitar. She has very short, fair hair, and the most piercing, palest blue eyes I have ever seen. She walks to Ric and sits next to him on his bed.

Neither of them look at each other, or acknowledge each other's presence, but as soon as they are sitting together it's like something is complete, like something that was broken has been fixed. Then she starts to play.

Angharad – I'm guessing this must be Angharad – plucks her strings softly and carefully, picking out a sweet and gentle melody that is both at odds with and in complement to Ric's harsh strumming. She harmonises his groaning song with a soothing humming, and their voices dance through the room, full of emotion and opposites and contradictions.

They seamlessly move from Ric's dark song to lighter songs; songs I know, and songs I've never heard. They sing about heaven and hell, love and revolution and redemption, and then Ric sings in his language and Angharad hums.

The mood changes again; Angharad plays harder, and the two guitars are battling, and then they drift back together. The air in the room seems to fill with electricity that makes my whole body tingle from the inside out, and I feel I am being allowed to watch something magical, but that I'm also intruding on something deeply personal.

I don't notice Pam in the room until she steps into view and I see her eyes are full of tears. She moves to Angharad, puts her hand on her shoulder and whispers something in her ear. Angharad stops playing and leaves.

Ric plays on by himself. His song gets darker, and louder, and more and more discordant until it is little more than a relentless din and I want to tell him to stop. I move to Saeed, who is sweating and trembling, thinking Ric might notice and calm his playing, but he carries on and I stare out of the window, searching for Debbie inside my head.

Eventually Ric slows down and a tune breaks out through the noise, and although he is still strumming angrily he starts to sing slowly and softly.

Show me peace
Amid the roar
Show me peace, show me peace
Find me waves
Along the shore
Show me peace, show me peace.

I can feel Debbie now. I know she is close.

Blow across the open sky
Show me peace before I die
Come for me with gentle song
Speak of good and not of wrong.

She is sitting on the window ledge, smiling, kicking her legs back and forth. Ric sings and she joins in, and I wonder if Ric can hear her too.

Show me peace
Among the waves
Show me peace, show me peace
Show me peace
Among the graves
Show me peace, show me peace.

The door opens and I know they have come for me.
I run towards them, and the wind rushes ahead of
me and smashes into them but one of them grabs
my arm as I push past, and a needle pierces my
skin and darkness covers everything.

CHAPTER TWENTY-TWO

I wake on the table. I knew I would.

Dr Stuart is flicking through her notes.

'Paul, can you hear me?'

The restraints are so tight it's difficult to breathe. I close my eyes and see Debbie.

'It has come to our attention that your medications are not proving as effective as we'd hoped. The monitors are still recording periods of uncontrolled brain activity.'

I hear light footsteps; Dr Epstein has arrived. I keep my eyes closed. I don't want to see his smile.

'Hello, Paul. Dr Stuart has explained why we need to do some more tests.' He's not asking a question. There is nothing I can say that will change their minds. Nothing I can say will stop this.

Debbie? Help me get out of here.

Oh happy day.

'Activity?'
    '88%. Prep 1 administered.'
    'Proceed with prep 2. Stand ready.'
Buffalo grab my arms, my legs; there must be
six of them at least. One of them injects cold and
wind surges across the table, lashes around the
room.
    The table is shaking and the buffalo are
straining to hold it down and Debbie is belting out
her song.

HE TAUGHT ME TO FIGHT.

I see her out of the corner of my eye. She is
moving towards Dr Stuart, her eyes glazed, her
hair floating.
    'Activity?'
    '190%. Rising.'
    'Inject H2.'
Debbie puts her face right in front of Dr
Stuart's.

AND HE TAUGHT ME TO PRAY.

'Still rising.'
    'Repeat.'

The whole room is shaking. Metal is clashing against metal. The restraints are loosening but the grip of the buffalo is tightening.

'Still ris –' Dr Stuart looks up and her hard, wrinkled face loosens, like she has lost control of all her muscles. A thin stream of blood trickles from her nose and she stares at Debbie, and Debbie stares back; eyes glazed, like in the pit.

'*DR STUART*, administer *H3. NOW.*'

I feel it this time, the darkness, the universe, and the wind dies down, but Debbie is still here. She is on the ceiling now, arms out, floating. There are stars between us, but wind too, and it whips the hair of the buffalo, lifts Dr Epstein's white coat as he struggles towards Dr Stuart and her tray of syringes.

A gust of wind flies from Debbie and blows the syringes across the floor; Dr Epstein falls to his hands and knees and scrambles around, shouting at Dr Stuart. I strain to sit up. I want to get up so badly but there are too many buffalo, all pressing down on me, and their weight is too much for me, too much for the wind.

Someone injects me again and I feel the darkness, stronger this time, like oil filling my body, filling the room. It engulfs Debbie, and the wind, so powerful before, now does nothing more than gently stir the sea of oil between us. I try to reach for her but I can't move my arms and the oil blocks everything. I can't see her anymore.

'3%.'

There is a long, silent pause. The oil gently sloshes, and the buffalo breathe heavily, but there is no talking, no singing, no Debbie.

'Holding steady.'

'Fine. Single dose of H4 twice daily. If his activity rises above 5%, administer a double dose.'

The buffalo remove the straps, lift me from the table, and pull me through the oil. They drag me along a corridor. The oil doesn't stop them. It washes over me, sticks to me. We pass windows with empty beds behind them and the buffalo swerve to avoid a door that has peeled back from its frame; a huge, solid metal door that has just curled into a roll. Through the window I see what used to be a bed. It is so warped and twisted it is barely recognisable. Tyrone, I think, Tyrone can help us get out of here. He bends things. Breaks things.

The buffalo put me on my bed, coated in oil. The room is full of oil, but I know Tyrone, with his angry eyebrows and his angry voices that bend and break things can help us get out of here, and it gives me hope, and that somehow makes it all right to be stuck in the oil.

CHAPTER
TWENTY-THREE

Ric is shouting, arguing. I open my eyes and sit up. Saeed's bed is empty, the sheets removed. Bars of sunlight fall from the blinds and stripe the bare mattress. Ric is behind his curtain. It's like he's talking to ten people at once and he's angry with all of them.

The door opens and I count the buffalo; Pam in front, four more behind. She gives Ric his pills and he takes them without argument, lies back on his bed and chants.

'Where's Saeed?' I ask as she approaches.

Pam frowns. 'They are doing everything they can.' She offers me a pot of pills and I ignore them. I feel anger rising fast.

Pam sighs. She looks tired, her eyes red. 'Look, Paul, I know you think this place is bad, but it's not. Everyone here works very hard to help the patients get better.'

'What they're doing here is *wrong*.' Debbie's words fly out of my mouth. Or Ric's words. I'm not sure. 'They lock us up, they test drugs on us, they put wires in our heads, and –' I look across at Saeed's empty bed, Ric's words about being pulled to pieces now running through my mind. 'Do you think this is all right? Do you think it would be all right by your "good Lord"?'

Pam's face hardens and she jabs a finger towards me. 'The good Lord knows our intentions are good, and that's what matters. We try very hard to help the children here. Some of them are extremely difficult; some might even say they have the devil in them.' She looks away, like she can't bear to look at my face, like maybe she saw the devil in me.

My mind races with thoughts of the devil, thoughts of possession, thoughts of evil spirits. Is that really what she thinks? Is that possible?

Pam turns back to me, her eyes softer. 'The children here need help, and we do everything we can to help them.' She holds out the pills again. 'Take them, Paul. Please.'

I look to the corridor; at the Buffalo gathering behind the door, Ric's chanting droning in the background, Saeed's bed swelling behind me with its emptiness, and I know this isn't the time to fight and I take the pills, and I hate myself for it.

Pam returns with a stack of trays and a huge bag of solid-looking grey stuff. She lays out six trays on the floor, where the table used to be before Tyrone bent it and they took it away. She opens the bag and wrenches great lumps off, and I realise it is clay.

'Ric,' she calls. He is still chanting on his bed. She glances up at me; she looks like she wants to smile, 'Come on, Paul, I told you it's not all bad in here.'

Like a lump of clay makes everything all right.

Ric moves to a tray, still chanting. He sits cross-legged in front of it and starts rolling his clay into a fat cylinder. I sit next to him and squeeze my piece of clay restlessly until Pam leaves.

'Where are the other wards, Ric?' I whisper.

He laughs and his eyes light up, 'Chief Red Cloud told me –'

'Are they all on this floor?'

Ric nods, 'Three wards, four isolation rooms, an operating theatre and a treatment room.'

'All on this floor?'

Ric nods again and smooths the sides of his cylinder; he has balanced it upright, like a pole. 'Downstairs are just offices and rooms for the staff.'

'How many staff?'

'Never more than ten at once, including the doctors, and usually less than that.' He laughs again. I think he's laughing at something one of his voices said. Then he goes all quiet and serious. 'We have to get Saeed out soon, he's in danger. And Angharad, we have to save Angharad. She can stop them.' He starts humming, distracted by his clay. He is shaping a face into the base of the cylinder. The door opens again; I count five buffalo outside the room.

Angharad comes in first. She sits next to Ric and they don't look at each other, don't talk to each other, but again there is that feeling that something has been fixed. Ric moves slower, calmer, and his smile looks contented instead of deranged. He gently works more shapes into his clay and Angharad rolls hers into a ball.

Madeline comes in next, giggling and flirting with Griff, who seems oblivious to her presence. Griff sees the clay and sits down, starts working it with his hands, a look of great concentration on his face.

Davis comes in last. He pulls his tray away from the rest of us, and sits right up against a wall, his gaze darting around the room as he crushes his clay between tense fingers.

The door closes and I look up. Three buffalo have stayed in the room with us. At least two are outside the door.

'Where's Tyrone?' I ask the room in general.

Griff is focused on his clay. Madeline smiles and shrugs her shoulders. Ric and Angharad are not really here; it's like they've built their own little world and are communicating on some other level far away from the rest of us.

I look at Davis, tense and twitchy against the wall. 'Davis, do you know where Tyrone is?'

'They took him this morning,' Davis whispers. 'He bent another bed.'

'It's really incredible what he can do, isn't it?' Madeline smiles.

I nod. It is, and I think it's going to help get us out of here.

'There will be a scientific explanation for it one day,' Madeline pushes her fingers into her clay, 'don't you think?'

'I guess so.'

'His spirits do it,' Ric says firmly. 'When they're angry.'

'It could be the power of his mind.' Madeline breaks her clay into two pieces.

'No. It's spirits.' Ric leans back and looks at his clay. I can see it's going to be a totem pole now, with an eagle on the top, wings outstretched.

'Do you hear spirits, Paul?' Madeline smiles at me. 'Or are they voices in your head?'

I look down at my clay, still a formless blob. 'I don't know.'

'He hears a spirit,' Ric stands and lifts his arms into the air, 'and she brings the wind.'

A buffalo moves towards Ric. He raises his fists and laughs. Angharad brushes his ankle with her fingertips; he sits down again and the buffalo moves back. Angharad carries on working her clay; pressing the shape of the continents into her ball using a fingernail.

'Did you lose someone close?' Madeline asks.

'I –' My eyes sting and I blink, fast.

'I don't mean to pry,' Madeline smiles, 'it's just the ones that lost someone close tend to think their voices are the person they lost. Maybe it's just grief, you know –'

'It's spirits,' Ric interrupts. 'I hear them. I know.'

Madeline looks at her clay, now broken into four separate pieces. 'I know you do, Ric, but maybe not all of us do. Maybe for some of us they are just voices in our head. The mind playing tricks. It's a powerful thing.'

'It's spirits.' Ric squashes a flat tail into the base of his totem pole. 'Powerful spirits. Spirits of people who died in turmoil. They want to control them, use them for their own gain.' He turns and stares at the buffalo.

'Hmm.' Madeline picks up one of her pieces of clay and starts breaking it into smaller and smaller pieces. 'You must admit that sounds a little paranoid, Ric.'

'You don't understand. They took your spirits away.' Ric looks at her with sad, sympathetic eyes.

'I was ill, Ric. I heard voices in my head. They found the right medication to control my condition.' Madeline's voice falters when she uses Dr Stuart's words. I wonder if she really believes them.

Ric grunts and presses more patterns into the back of his totem pole.

Madeline straightens her back and glances over at Griff. 'They helped Griff, too. They are going to let us out soon.'

'They will never let you out.' Ric looks at Madeline, his face a thundercloud. 'If you aren't useful to them they –'

'Oh please, Ric. Don't talk about dissecting again.' Madeline turns to me, 'You don't believe him, do you, Paul? You know how ridiculous it sounds.'

I want to believe Madeline, and Pam. I want to believe the doctors here are trying to help, but everything just feels so wrong.

Ric carefully puts his totem pole down on his tray. 'They did it to Tom.'

Madeline's eyes flash with anger and pain. 'They did not. They let Tom out. I'm going to see him when I get out of here.'

'Chief –'

Madeline stands up and glares at Ric. 'Chief somebody sent you a vision. It's all in your head, Ric. Your sick, messed up head. Tom is fine. They cured him and let him out, and they are going to let me out, too.'

I stare at Madeline. She seems to be getting

bigger and it takes me a moment to realise she is rising from the floor. A line of red trickles from her eye, down her cheek. Blood. A buffalo rushes to her, grabs her in his arms, and carries her to the door. Another one walks alongside, fumbling with a needle.

The door closes. Ric jumps up and flies at the last buffalo left in the room, and smashes him into the floor. Before I have a chance to think about what is happening, Angharad leans over to me and touches the wires on either side of my head, just a finger to each one, and I feel a surge of electricity move along the wires and into my brain, and it's the strangest sensation I've ever felt, like popping candy is bursting and echoing inside my skull. She whispers close to my ear, 'Now they won't know when she comes,' and then leans back and picks up her clay as more buffalo rush into the room.

In an instant there is chaos. Buffalo pile onto Ric and inject him and the lights above us start to flicker, and I think I see sparks flashing out of Angharad's fingers. A buffalo lifts her up and takes her away, and more buffalo arrive. One goes to pick up Davis. He has retreated to a corner and is all small and tight, knees up to his chest. Like Debbie when she is upset.

Griff is staring into the distance, eyes glazed, like Debbie's when she lay in the pit, and it occurs to me that they are all like Debbie. Ric has her words, her songs. He taunts me, confuses me, like

Debbie. Madeline has her smile. She is playful. Davis has her fear, Tyrone has her anger, Saeed has her innocence, and Angharad is calming. They are all like Debbie, and maybe that is why I need to get them out of here.

Buffalo take Davis and Griff away and lift Ricardo onto his bed. He is sweating, bruised and chanting under his breath. I put his totem pole on the windowsill next to his bed and look at the rest of the clay scattered across the floor. Angharad's perfect world. Davis's piece, crushed into a mould of his fist by tense hands. Madeline's clay, torn into tiny pieces. My formless blob. Griff's work catches my eye and I pick it up. It is a flat tablet, concentric circles drawn into the clay, a jagged line like lightning smashing into it.

CHAPTER TWENTY-FOUR

A surge of wind expands through the darkness and pulls me from my sleep. I open my eyes expecting to see Debbie, but she isn't here, and the noise of the wind isn't right; it's rhythmic, thumping. A dazzling beam of light hits the window and the blinds slice it into white bands that run across the room. I step out of bed, walk to the window, and stare out into the darkness.

A helicopter, huge and black behind the light, is coming in to land. The rotor blades pound the air, the beam of light swings down onto the grass, and the helicopter lurches to the ground. The blades slow, a high pitched whine fills the air, and the beam disappears, engulfed by the darkness. I suddenly see my reflection in the glass, the wires sticking out of my head, and I feel sick.

A weak, yellow light flicks on outside the house and Dr Stuart walks out, followed by a couple of buffalo. Two men descend from the helicopter and walk into the light. The first man is tall, hard-faced and muscular, wearing a black uniform. The second man, wearing a white coat, is Dr Epstein.

'Tŷ Eidolon.' Ric is standing next to me. I didn't hear him get out of bed.

'What?'

'They've come from Tŷ Eidolon.' Ric points at the hard-faced man in the black uniform. 'He comes to take patients away.' The doctors, the buffalo and the hard-faced man all walk into the house and the light flicks off.

'Tŷ Eidolon?' I remember Dr Epstein saying I would be transferred to Tŷ Eidolon. He said I would go there once the medications were working. To start a new life.

'They only send some there. The ones they think will be useful to them. The ones that make fire, or ice, or move things with their mind, or read your thoughts, or –'

'How do you know?'

'I've seen it. I know.'

The yellow light flicks back on and two buffalo walk out, carrying someone small in a yellow uniform. She has long, dark hair and a pretty face. Madeline is out cold. The buffalo lift her into the helicopter and Dr Epstein climbs in after her. The hard-faced man strides out of the house and steps in last. Before he shuts the door, he looks up at our window. He stares right at me, and a sharp pain pierces the centre of my forehead. I stare back at him and I know he is all kinds of wrong.

The helicopter blades drum the air and Ric walks back to his bed, his shoulders hunched, his face solemn.

'Maybe they're letting her go.' I say it but I know it's not true. Why would she be drugged if they were letting her go? Why would they take her away in a helicopter in the middle of the night?

'It's my fault.' Ric stares at the light swerving away into the darkness. 'I provoked her. I wanted a distraction so Angharad could short circuit your monitors. I shouldn't have talked about Tom. She got too upset, and then she levitated and now they think she's useful.'

'Madeline levitated,' I whisper. It had all happened so fast I wasn't sure it was real. Saying the words out loud makes it feel true.

'I didn't know. I thought they had taken her spirits away.' Ric stands, his voice rises, and he starts ranting, 'They find ways to control your spirits, and if they can't, if you aren't useful to them then they tests drugs on you, more and more, until you fall apart like Griff, and then eventually they pull you to pieces like Tom.'

'How can you know that?' I don't want to believe him.

'I've seen it.' Ric shouts. '*I'VE SEEN IT.*' His

eyes look wild, crazy. Has he seen it for real, or in his head? Has he found out the truth, or is he paranoid, like Madeline said?

Ric starts chanting, louder and louder, more and more discordant, until I can't take it anymore and I walk over to his bed and draw the curtain around him. I go to my bed, pull the curtain around it too, and squeeze my eyes shut to try and block out Ric and his thoughts. Why would they kill patients, why would they dissect them? It makes no sense. I don't want it to make sense. I feel blood draining from my face, sinking down my neck into my stomach, and I feel faint. I wish Debbie was here. I close my eyes and search for her. If I can find her she will know the answers. She will know what to do.

I am lying on sand, water lapping at my feet. I sit up and look across the beach, to Tom's bed.

'Tom that is gone,' Saeed whispers.

A boy is sitting on Tom's bed. He is about my age, thin, with long, curly hair. He's wearing the yellow overalls of a patient. He stands and walks towards me, moving slowly and carefully; he has a quiet composure and a peaceful face, but his hands tremble in a medical way, a way that makes me think of the drugs they've given him.

He sits in front of me, looks me in the eyes.

'Paul.' He smiles hesitantly. 'I'm Tom.' His voice wavers, like his hands.

'Are you dead?' I ask.

The water washes onto the sand and Tom looks at the ocean out of the window with tranquil eyes. He lifts a hand, his fingers quivering, and we are in a white room, an operating theatre. Antiseptic fumes sting my nose; gather in the back of my throat. There is a figure lying under a sheet on a cold, steel table in the middle of the room. Tom moves to the sheet and I freeze. He pulls it back with his trembling fingers and the sheet flows to the floor, and I try to look away but I can't.

There is a body on the table, pale and lifeless. It takes me a moment to realise it's Tom. His long, curly hair is gone and there are fresh, bloodless scars on his head, stitched up crudely with thick, dark thread. He is pale, empty, like a wax model. No blood is flowing in his veins. His fingers, grey and cracked, lie still on the metal.

I feel sick. I turn away and there is another table in front of me, another body. I turn again and another table rises up, another body. Soon I am surrounded by them, and there is no way out. I squeeze my eyes shut and I see Saeed, lying still on the table; a thinner version of him, his skin tight across his skull.

I squeeze my eyes tighter. I put my hands over my head. It's just a dream. This is just a dream. It's not real. It can't be. I fall to my knees and sink into the sand, deeper and deeper. It tightens around me. Something grabs my arms and sucks my strength away and the black ocean washes over me and I let it carry me away. I keep my eyes tight shut and I drift far, far away.

CHAPTER TWENTY-FIVE

Pam walks in carrying a fresh bundle of sheets and starts making up Tom's bed. Davis is behind her, his small body tense, his eyes flitting as he tracks unseen shadows across the walls.

'Where's Tom?' I ask, last night's dream still lingering in my mind.

Pam tucks a corner of a sheet under the mattress and ignores my question. 'Davis has been moved to your ward instead.'

'Is Tom dead?'

Pam turns to me. 'I can tell you've been listening to Ric's nonsense. Don't believe what he says, Paul. He's a paranoid schizophrenic; that's why he's in here. Don't obsess over matters that don't concern you.'

'Is Tom dead?' My voice is rising. I can't help

it. 'Where's Saeed? Have they killed him, too?'

Two more buffalo step into the room and move towards my bed. I stare at them. My eyes are burning, my fists clenched.

'Paul.' Pam's voice is forcibly calm. 'Nobody has killed anybody. You're getting yourself all worked up for no reason. You need to focus on your own health.'

'I just want to know where Saeed is. Is he dead?'

Pam looks out of the window. A buffalo grabs my arm and without thinking I throw a punch, and it smashes into his jaw. He reels back and I feel a needle pierce my thigh. Suddenly everything goes cloudy and soft and warm and I am aware of being gently lowered onto my bed. I hear voices but no words, footfalls bouncing up from the floor and down from the ceiling. Another needle stabs into my arm, the curtain rings slide across the rail high above my head, and black water washes over my body.

'Pablo?' Ric is leaning over me. I can feel his smile shining through the air. 'Pablo, wake up.' He slaps my face softly, persistently, like how I used to knock on Debbie's door.

I hear a groan. I think it is me. 'What?' My voice is rough and my head is heavy, as if it is filled with sand.

'You have to hear this. Get up.'

I sit up and slide my legs out of bed. The room spins, pitches sideways, and then swings into focus.

'Tell him, Davis.' Ric gallops across the room. His yellow overalls are tied around his waist and his tattoos seem to have multiplied. Every inch of his skin is covered in scrawls and I can't remember if they were all there before.

Davis is sitting on Tom's bed. He looks over to me but gets distracted by something. His gaze drifts across the window and he shuffles back on the bed, pulls his knees tight to his chest. I walk over and sit next to him.

'Are you all right, Davis?'

'Paul?' he says quietly, still staring at the window.

'Yes,' I nod.

'Can you see them?'

'What?'

'The shadows.'

I look around and shake my head. 'No.'

Davis takes a breath, a small sigh of relief.

'They're looking for a way out.' Ric turns to the door.

'What?' I ask.

'Davis's spirits.'

'Ric sees my shadows, too.' Davis looks me right in the eyes and I can see the strain on his face, the effort it's taking for him to stay focused on just me. 'It's fine if Ric sees them, but if you see them it's bad.'

'Why?'

'Because then maybe they would see them too,' he glances at the window to the corridor, 'the wardens and the doctors, and then they'd do more tests.' Davis hugs his knees. 'I don't like the tests.'

'Tell him,' Ric beams, 'tell him about Griff.'

'Griff has disappeared,' Davis whispers.

Ric laughs. He is smiling his excited, manic smile, and I don't understand why he looks so happy with this news.

'Last night,' Davis leans close to me, 'he was in his bed and then he wasn't.'

'His spirits are powerful.' Ric jumps up, fists waving in the air. 'They have saved him; transported him, or made him invisible, or –' Ric's eyes gleam with excitement, 'moved him through time.'

I shake my head. 'The doctors have taken him somewhere.'

'No, you don't understand.' Davis is looking right at me and I can see he has something important he wants to say. 'He disappeared, vanished, there one moment, gone the next, and the doctors don't know where he is.'

'How do you know?'

'One of my shadows got downstairs last night.'

'One of your shadows?'

'That's what they do.' Davis's focus drifts away as he follows something across the walls. 'They move around. Sometimes they find a way out and then I see what they see and hear what they hear. One of them got downstairs last night and heard the doctors talking. Dr Epstein and the other man were angry with Dr Stuart because she didn't know where Griff was.'

I think about the helicopter last night, about Dr Epstein, and the man with the hard face and the painful stare.

'Dr Epstein and the man took Madeline to Tŷ Eidolon.'

I nod.

'They want to take Tyrone and you next. Dr Stuart said she has a few more tests to do first. I don't like the tests.'

'What do you know about Tŷ Eidolon?'

'I think it might be a good place,' Davis ventures. 'I heard them talk about training, and dormitories, and how you could be useful.' Davis points to one of Ric's tattoos, the one with the ring of concentric circles and the lightning smashing into it. 'Something like that was on the man's sleeve, but just the circles.'

'They want to control the spirits, they –' Ric starts ranting but stops abruptly and looks at Davis like he just remembered something else. 'Tell him about Saeed.'

'My shadow saw Saeed in an isolation room the

147

night before last. Angharad, Tyrone and Saeed were all in isolation rooms.'

'And Saeed was all right?'

'I think so. He was asleep.'

'It's a sign,' Ric beams, 'from the spirits. The time is right. The time is now. We have to save Saeed and Angharad. Get everyone out before they send you to Tŷ Eidolon.' He slaps me hard on the back. 'Pablo will free us and Angharad will stop them.'

Davis's eyes widen and his face pales beneath his bright red hair. Even his freckles seem to fade. 'I don't want to leave.'

Ric stares at him like he is crazy.

'They are trying to help,' Davis looks up at me, 'aren't they, Paul?'

I don't know what to say.

'I don't like the tests, but they do it to help. Without the medicines the shadows and the voices are worse. I need the medicines to get better.'

I don't know what to say. Davis is scared of his voices, like Saeed. Maybe they are better off here; maybe the doctors will help them. I look at Ric and his manic smile and his body covered in scrawls that make no sense and all of a sudden I feel so lost and confused. I don't know what to believe. I don't know what is real and what is delusion – or illusion. I wish Debbie was here. She would know what to do, she would make sense.

The door opens and Pam walks in, carrying

three pots of pills. Ric goes to his bed and starts chanting, slow and melancholy. He takes his pills without argument, and Davis does too, and then Pam is stood in front of me, holding out the pills that stop Debbie from coming.

'Please,' I say. 'I'm sorry about earlier. I need to see Debbie.'

'It's not healthy to dwell in the past, Paul. You have to move forwards. Move on.'

'I know,' I nod, 'and I know she is slipping away from me, and I just want to see her one last time to say goodbye.'

Pam's eyes soften and I see I have reached her. A little bit of her understands, and perhaps it's that, or perhaps because she thinks the monitors work and the buffalo can come whenever they want and inject me with the darkness, she slips the pills in her pocket and walks away.

CHAPTER TWENTY-SIX

'Wakey wakey, Paul.'

I open my eyes. It's dark, but I can make her out. She is sitting on the window ledge, strumming the blinds. I am so relieved to see her all I can think about is getting out, right now, with her. I can't let them take her away again.

We have to get out of here.

'I know.' She jumps off the window ledge and boxes the air. 'Spar with me, Paul.'

I get out of bed and walk to her. She looks so real. So completely real.

'I am real.' She throws a punch and I duck out of the way.

Don't confuse me.

'It doesn't take much, Paulie.'

I can smell her hair.

Are you a ghost?

'What do you think?' She throws another punch and I duck again.

I don't know.

'Come on, Paul, there must be some smarts in that fat, wired head of yours.'

Shut up.

I smile. Debbie is back, and the buffalo haven't come. Angharad was right. They don't know she's here.

'Come on, Paulie, throw a punch.'

No.

She looks at me and all of a sudden everything makes sense. What they are doing here is wrong, and I have to get everyone out. I have to protect them, to make up for not protecting Debbie. I have to get it right this time, or there is nothing of me.

'The wards don't have proper locks; just bolts. If you get to the other side of that door, you can open up all the wards.'

I think Tyrone can help. He can bend things.

'You don't know what state Tyrone will be in.'

I guess not. I don't know what state anyone will be in.

The sky is lightening, the first beams of sunlight breaking through the blinds.

They'll come soon, with drugs to push you away.

'It doesn't matter.' Debbie boxes the air. 'You are stronger than them, and their drugs. Spar with me, Paul.'

152

I put my fists up. She smiles, and her eyes change. They are not happy, they are never happy, but they aren't glazed anymore. They have life in them. Her cheeks are flushed, her hair is bouncing. I throw a punch and she is too slow to dodge it, but I stop before I hit her. My hand hovers over her cheek; I want to touch her, to see if she is real. She looks so real…

She laughs and pulls away, throws a punch and I duck.

I have Debbie back, and I'm not letting them take her away again. We are going to get out of here, together.

Ric pulls his curtain back, smiling wide, looking from me to Debbie. 'Pablo,' he nods, 'we're going to get out of here,' and he beams at Debbie and he sings.

Oh happy day.

Debbie joins in, her sweet powerful voice ringing out over Ric's gravelly tones.

Oh happy day.

The door heaves open and I see two buffalo carrying pills. Anger explodes inside me, bursts out of me, and I run at them. I am not taking their pills anymore. I am not waiting any longer, I don't care that I have no plan; I am going to get out of here. I am going to fight my way out of here right now.

I punch one and he reels back. The other one grabs me from behind and I pull back my elbow sharply, digging it up and into his stomach. His grip loosens and Ric jumps on him, yelling with excitement. They fall to the floor and I feel the wind blow across my face. The blinds are swinging into the room.

'Get the door!' Debbie shouts.

I push my way past the first buffalo and catch the door before it shuts. The buffalo grabs me as he loses balance, and pulls me down with him. I tense all my muscles and try to stand firm, but he is like a great boulder collapsing onto me. He traps my arms and the door is going to shut.

'Ric!' I shout. He dives towards the door. The buffalo that was under him rises to his knees and reaches for Ric's ankle, but he doesn't get a grip. Ric jumps onto the buffalo on top of me and I'm crushed into the floor, but Ric has made it to the door and he is pulling it open.

The buffalo on top of me wrenches my arms back, pins me down with a knee and I am struggling, really struggling to move. Suddenly, his head jerks back and I break free. Debbie is standing over him. She pulls her arm back and she punches him again, hard, and his nose bleeds. He stares at her in shock. I push past him and move to the door but I see Davis out of the corner of my eye, huddled back on his bed, not moving; just staring at us all in shock and confusion.

'Come on!' I shout, but he just sits there, frozen.

The wind surges towards the buffalo between us and they skid across the floor, raising their arms to shield their faces from the blast. I rush to Davis, pick him up and throw him over my shoulder, run back to the door and step into the corridor. I put Davis down as the buffalo rise to their feet and Ric starts pulling the door shut.

The buffalo lunge, reaching for the door through the wind but it surges into a gale and they can't push through it. They struggle towards us but the door is closing. It slams shut and Ric pulls the bolts across, sealing the buffalo in. Ric turns to me, smiling and laughing louder than the wind.

I look down at Davis, right into his eyes. 'Focus on staying with us, OK?'

He nods, Ric grabs my arm and pulls me to the left and we run down the corridor, Davis following close behind.

We pass the window to the isolation room I was in. The blinds are still scattered across the floor, the bed empty. We keep running and pass another window; the room with the twisted bed. An alarm wails through the air.

Three buffalo round the corner ahead of us and Ric rushes towards them, his war cry screaming above the alarm. I run at them too, past Ric, and the wind rushes with me and I crash into the buffalo. One of them falls to the floor and I fall with him, punching and punching, but I feel another one, grabbing and pulling, and I see him fiddling with something and I realise it's a syringe.

'Debbie!' I call, but she is there already. She kicks the syringe out of his hand and his nose bleeds and his face runs pale. The wind whirls around us, crushing and stinging. A cyclone is forming in the corridor, and I scramble to my feet and back away from the buffalo.

One of them runs at me, tackles me, his huge mass slamming me into the floor. I struggle and kick. My leg breaks free and I kick him on the shoulder; I think he is letting go when another buffalo lands on my back, forcing the air from my lungs. I try and wrestle my arms free, but I am getting nowhere. I start to panic. They can't beat me, not now.

The wind gets faster and louder but the buffalo aren't moving. I hear Debbie shout, I hear her landing punches on them, but I am still trapped. I close my eyes and tense all my muscles. I am going to get up. They can't beat me now. I try and lift my body, I try and lift it with all my strength but the buffalo aren't budging. They are like a mountain of rock on top of me.

I hear bolts sliding back. I turn my head and see Ric opening a door, Angharad stepping out. The lights flicker off and sparks rain down from the ceiling. A sheet of lightning flashes down the corridor, so bright it blinds me. I can't see, but I can move again. I push the buffalo off and fight my way to my feet. It's dark, and it smells of burning.

The lights flicker back on. All three buffalo are on the floor, near the door, struggling to their feet.

'Hold it open!' I shout to Ric.

Ric pushes the door open further and the wind surges. It rolls towards the buffalo in a great tidal wave, hammering them back. They skid towards the door. Ric grabs them and hauls them through into the isolation room. All I can hear is the wind. It forces the buffalo back, further and further into the room, and we pull the door closed and bolt it.

The wind dies down a little; it's still roaring, but I can hear the alarm again now, and Ric laughing and shouting. I look around. We have Angharad and Davis, but we still need Saeed and Tyrone.

I run down the corridor and Ric follows close behind. We round a corner, and there are double doors on our right with no bolts, no lock. We push past them and the wind stops. Ric's laughter stops. Everything but the alarm stops. The alarm keeps on wailing.

We are in a white room, an operating theatre, and there is a small figure under a sheet on a table in the middle of the room. A cold wave rolls through me.

Ric moves towards the sheet and I grab his arm without thinking. I don't want him to look. If nobody looks it won't be true. Ric shrugs me off and steps to the sheet, unflinching, unshakeable, and I turn around. I turn back to the door.

Heavy footsteps are pounding down the corridor. More buffalo are coming. I open the doors and step through. I am going to beat them all, and I am going to burn this place down.

CHAPTER TWENTY-SEVEN

The doors swing shut behind me. Angharad fixes her eyes on me and I look away. Two buffalo are running towards us. Angharad steps forward, and a bolt of lightning flashes down from the ceiling amid a shower of sparks and smoke.

The wind picks up and my heart beats faster and faster, until it pounds in my chest and blood surges around my body, hot and corrosive. I storm towards the buffalo and the wind bursts ahead of me. They are weak and they are flapping in the wind and I will take them down.

I punch and I punch, and they fall back. One of them hits me but I don't feel it. The other forces an arm around my neck, tries to fix me in a headlock, but I swipe back with my leg, throw him off balance, and he falls to the floor. They are weak, and a hurricane is building in this corridor. They don't stand a chance. Wind pushes them to the floor. I punch, again and again, until they lie there unmoving, and there is no reason to go on.

I stand and look at them; unconscious, useless, broken. My chest is heaving, my lungs burning. Angharad touches my arm and I flinch. Davis is behind her, but Ric is not. He must still be in the operating theatre.

I open the doors, but I can't look in.

'Ric,' I shout, but my voice is overwhelmed by the alarm.

Angharad steps into the room and I feel relieved. I let the door swing shut after her and I walk on, down the corridor. I step over the buffalo and pass the window of an empty room, then another window. Someone is in the bed behind it. Tyrone.

I heave the door open and shout to him, but there is no response. Davis holds the door for me and I go to him, pick him up. He is out cold, the sort of out cold that comes from too much medicine.

I carry him around the next corner and there is the door, the door to the stairs. We are going to get out of here. I look at the lock, and I look at Tyrone. Still out cold. I place him on the floor and start kicking the door.

I think about Saeed. I think about the wires. I think about the medicines, and I kick and I kick, again and again. The door shakes, creaks, but it does not give.

Debbie? Help me.

I TAUGHT HIM TO FIGHT AND I TAUGHT HIM TO PRAY.

I run at the door, throw my body at it, but it still doesn't give. I take a few steps back, ready to barge it again but then I hear it creaking, see it folding and splitting. The whole door is crumpling in on itself. The lock bends and snaps. I look at Tyrone. His eyes are open, his eyebrows furrowed. He is staring at the door and I can hear his voices; angry shouts and screams of despair.

The door breaks off its hinges and crumples, tighter and tighter, smaller and smaller until it is a ball of mangled metal in a cloud of dust. We are going to get out of here.

I look around for Ric. He rounds the corner, walking tall, hardened and impenetrable. Angharad is with him but nothing is fixed. Nothing can make this right.

I run down the stairs and smash through the doors at the bottom. They burst open and I fly into a hall. One door left and we are outside.

One door left and Pam is in front of it, her arms folded over her chest. I walk to her, look her in the eye. She looks right back at me and raises a finger to my chest. 'You can't take these children out of here. They are ill and they need help.'

'What goes on here is *WRONG*,' I shout, '*THEY KILLED SAEED*.'

Pam lowers her shoulders, softens a little. 'That was nobody's fault, child, he had an infection. They did everything they could.'

The wind rises. I want to push her out of the way. My fists are clenched, my arms tense. 'How did he get an infection? From the wires they put in his head?'

She looks at the floor.

The wind gusts around her, but she holds herself firm.

'Paul,' she looks up at me, 'if you take these children out of here, their lives will be in *YOUR* hands. Do you want that after what happened to Debbie?'

Debbie. Debbie is here and I need to get her out before I lose her again. I need to get everyone out. This time I need to do what is right.

The wind dies down and Debbie appears, right in front of Pam, hair floating, like in the pit. Pam moves her hand over her mouth and her eyes fill with tears. Debbie sings and Pam falls to her knees, clutching the crucifix around her neck and mumbling prayers to her good Lord.

We are getting out of here. Right now. I turn back to the door and the wind smashes it open. Ric leads Angharad, Tyrone and Davis out and I follow, and the wind slams the door shut after me.

CHAPTER TWENTY-EIGHT

We walk away from Tŷ Hapus. Happy House. A hurricane is roaring around it, battering the walls, rattling the windows. Ric, Angharad, Tyrone and Davis disappear into the woods, but I pause at the edge of the line of trees and look back. No one has come out. No one is following us. Will they just let us go?

'What do you think, Paulie?'

No. We aren't free, we aren't safe.

'So you do have a few smarts, then?'

Shut up.

I stare at the building and wind surges towards it.

I'm going to destroy this place.

'What's the point, Paulie?' Debbie leans against a tree. 'Will it make you feel safe?'

It will make me feel better.

'Really?'

Really.

I think of Saeed, and of the medicines. I think of the tests they did, and of the wires in my head. I remember how they buried Debbie in rocks, how they drowned her in black water, how they engulfed her in oil, and the wind rises.

I feel something touch my shoulder and I whip round, fist raised, and have to stop myself striking because it is Angharad.

'What are you doing?' Angharad looks across to the house. 'Let's go.'

'I want to destroy this place.'

Angharad smiles and starts whispering. I hear her voices whispering back; two of them, young girls, like her. Something moves behind her and I think I see another girl, a girl with pale blue eyes like Angharad, but she disappears when I try to focus on her.

The air fills with electricity. It shivers across my skin. Sheets of lightning flash across the sky towards the house and the whispers get louder. A bolt of lightning strikes the roof and sends tiles crashing to the ground. Another flash, and another, and sparks fly from the light above the door and smoke curls in the air.

'How are you doing that?'

She just smiles, her face glowing.

I think of the doctors; of Dr Stuart's

condescending frown and Dr Epstein's sympathetic smile, and wind slams into the house. Windows shake and shatter, walls tremble and crumble, debris flies through the air. A storm surrounds the house, pummels it, lightning keeps flashing, sparks and smoke rise into the air.

The doctors and the buffalo leave the building. They gather in the clearing in front of it and watch as flames lick out of windows and smoke billows into the air. The fire grows, surrounds and consumes the building. Clouds of smoke and soot and ash drift towards us and I smell it, thick and acrid. The buffalo move further away, closer to us, and I turn to Debbie and Angharad.

'Let's go,' I whisper.

Angharad nods and I follow her into the woods.

'Feel better now, Paulie?' Debbie is jogging alongside me.

I glance back at the flames and smoke rising in the air. I don't feel better at all. It's just a building burning; it solves nothing. The doctors, the buffalo, the hard-faced man; they'll all carry on their work somewhere else. Tŷ Eidolon, where they were going to send me. We are not safe. We are not safe at all.

We catch up with Ric and Tyrone and Davis and walk further away from Tŷ Hapus, deeper into the woods, until the wind is calm, and the air is still, and the sound of the alarm has faded to a faint ringing in my ears. I start to hear outside noises,

noises I haven't heard in years. Twigs cracking underfoot, leaves rustling, birds singing. When I look up to the tree tops I feel dizzy, like my eyes have forgotten how to focus on things so far away, like my brain has forgotten how to interpret the size of the outside world.

I try to think how many years have passed since the funeral. The last time I was outside. The wind sweeping between the gravestones. Earth falling on her coffin. I blink, fast, to try and stop the tears. Two years, maybe three. I don't know anymore.

Ric is walking in front like he knows where he is going, and Angharad is walking alongside him. Davis is in her shadow, head down, arms wrapped around his chest, and Tyrone is further back. He is muttering under his breath, kicking at leaves, his movements jerky, angry.

And Debbie is walking next to me, singing joyfully.

Oh happy day
Oh happy day
I taught him to fight and I taught him to pray
Oh happy day.

Stop it. Please.
Debbie stops singing, 'What?'
I can't think.
'What do you need to think about?'
Where to go. What to do.

'Ric looks like he knows where he's going.'

I jog to catch up with Ric. He is bouncing along, talking to his voices. 'Ric, do you know where you're going?'

Ric ignores me, carries on talking in his language.

I touch his elbow. 'Ric, do you know where you're going?'

He turns to me and smiles wide. His manic smile. 'Trust the spirits, Pablo. They will protect us, show us the way.'

Ric bounds on, and I stop and look for Debbie. She is climbing onto a low branch of a tree off to my left.

'Do you have another plan, Paulie?'

I turn full circle. Trees, as far as I can see.

I don't. Is anyone following us?

Debbie jumps off the branch and skips over to me. 'What do you think?'

I don't know. They will, won't they?

'Spar with me, Paul.'

No.

Debbie sighs, turns away and sings.

He taught me how to watch
And to fight and pray
And to live rejoicing every day.

I try to ignore her. I try to focus on the sounds of the forest but Debbie is singing, and Ric is talking

167

to his voices, and Tyrone is muttering angry and their noises engulf me, suffocate me. I can't think straight, my head is filled with their din.

Hours pass in a blur of noise and confusion. The light grows orange as the sun begins to set and I realise we are heading west, towards the ocean. I could see it from the window in the isolation room. I wonder if there will be a beach, or a harbour. Maybe there will be a boat and we could sail away...

'You get angry, don't you?'

I turn to Angharad. She is walking next to me, calm and peaceful, like she is out for an evening stroll. I'm not sure what to say. I have a right to be angry. Don't I?

'You get angry,' she states simply. 'That's how you make your ghosts work.'

I don't know what to say to that, either. Debbie could be a ghost. I don't know.

'Saeed's ghost,' she breathes out slowly, 'used to make noise when he got scared. My ghosts make electricity when I want to help people, and your ghosts, they move the air when you get angry, don't they?'

'You think they are ghosts?'

Angharad nods. 'What else could they be?'

'They could all just be in our heads.'

'Do you think your voices are just in your head?'

I look at Debbie, sitting on a branch above me,

humming her song. 'I don't know. I don't understand any of this.' And that's the truth.

'Tyrone's voices are angry. Are your voices angry, too?'

'No.' Debbie is not angry, not all the time. She's just Debbie.

Angharad walks on in silence and I am glad she has stopped talking, stopped asking questions.

'My ghosts are my sisters,' she whispers after a while. 'I like having them close.' Her fingers brush my hand, and a mellow shock shivers up my arm. 'Thank you for getting us out.'

The sound of a helicopter pounds the air. It surges towards us, then away. I can't see it through the canopy, but I can tell it has come from the direction of the coast and is heading towards Tŷ Hapus. As the noise of it fades away I hear Ric, his voice louder, excited; having a dozen frenzied conversations all at once.

'Do you think Ric's voices are ghosts, too?'

'Some of them,' Angharad smiles, 'and the ones that are can create worlds.' She jogs over to him and puts her hand on his shoulder and he stops abruptly, stops, and smiles at Angharad, like all his voices have disappeared, or he has just chosen to ignore them all in favour of Angharad.

It's peaceful without Ric's ranting. Debbie is humming softly and Tyrone has stopped muttering altogether. I feel his anger, hot and prickly around his tense body. Davis's eyes flit to every shadow.

They are getting thicker and darker, the air growing cooler; a cold blackness gradually surrounding us. Davis looks exhausted. Everyone looks tired, everyone except Ric. He keeps moving forwards, a look of determination and sureness on his face that I envy. I wish I knew what I was doing.

'Spar with me, Paul.' Debbie boxes the air in front of me.

No. I need to think.

'What do you need to think about?'

Where to go. What to do.

'I thought you were following Ric.'

'We need water, food and shelter. A safe place to go.'

'What's your plan, Paulie?'

Maybe we should go to the police.

'That's the best you can come up with? You broke everyone out to hand them over to the police?' Debbie throws a punch and I duck out of the way.

It can't be legal, what they were doing in that place. The police would investigate it, and they would find us somewhere to go, somewhere safe. Wouldn't they?

'Maybe; or maybe they would send you to another Tŷ Hapus. Maybe they would send you to Tŷ Eidolon.'

Well what do you suggest, Debbie? *I DON'T KNOW WHAT TO DO.*

The wind picks up and Angharad turns to me, 'Are you all right, Paul?'

I nod a lie.

'I'm thirsty,' Tyrone scowls.

'Maybe we should look for a stream?' Angharad glances around, like there might be one nearby we haven't noticed.

Ric disappears into the trees ahead.

'This is stupid.' Tyrone sits down and glares at a fallen branch in front of him. It cracks, and the noise of it goes on and on, getting louder, until I see the branch folding, splintering, breaking into pieces. Angharad sits next to him and watches the branch disintegrate. 'None of you know where we're going.' Tyrone's voice rises and a long, dark shadow falls across us.

I look up. The trees are bending over us, further and further down. An intense creaking rolls through the air and I feel pressure bearing down on us. One of the trees is going to split, break and fall.

'Tyrone!' I shout, but he just closes his eyes and the noise carries on. His face is red; his eyebrows bearing down like the trees. A deafening crack tears through the air, and I pick Tyrone up, look into his screwed up face. 'Tyrone,' I try to speak calmly, 'you have to stop.' The ground is going to give; a tree is going to fall. I look up; I have to figure out which way to run.

'Listen,' Angharad puts her fingers on Tyrone's shoulder. 'Tyrone, do you hear that?'

Tyrone opens his eyes and the pressure eases.

I hear drums in the distance, the noise rolling rhythmically towards us.

Ric appears and beckons us onwards, 'Come and see,' he smiles.

I put Tyrone down and we follow Ric through the trees to a clearing. In the centre of it is a tipi; enormous and rising into the sky like a three storey building.

The poles are whole tree trunks, and a herd of cattle must have been killed to make the cover. Figures and symbols are painted all over it, made of simple shapes and lines, just like Ric's tattoos; eagles, arrows, suns, life-sized horses ... The thought occurs to me, that this is all just an illusion, but I push it away because I want this place to be real.

CHAPTER TWENTY-NINE

The tipi is empty, just a vast, open space with a few dormant features: a fireplace, a drum, a great skull with horns at the base of a stout centre pole, rugs and cushions, and animal hides around the periphery.

The symbols on the cover are huge, in silhouette, and they cast warped shadows across the compacted dirt floor. A diamond symbol catches my eye and I remember Ric's tattoo, the one he said was me. This place isn't real. It can't be. But I want it to be, and I think the others do too. They sit on cushions around the fireplace, a small mound of ash and charcoal, and I feel them relaxing, the doubt and tension in the air ebbing away.

Ric sits cross-legged and stares at the fireplace.

A thin stream of smoke curls up from the ashes to an open flap in the tipi high above us. The sound of drums in the distance moves closer. Flames rise from the ashes and crackle into the air, sparks dance around us. Ric chants quietly and it gradually gives way to a slow, gentle song, and Angharad joins in.

Their voices are soft and quiet, but they impact hard and reach my core before they float off into the woods harmoniously. They are both smiling, happy, and for the first time since we left Tŷ Hapus, since Saeed died, it feels as though Ric is all right again; not fixed, but not broken, not manic, not armoured.

They move from songs I understand to warm and mellow songs in Ric's foreign tongue and I realise I don't know where he is from or how he ended up here. Ric sings his song, the one I heard on the ward, and Angharad sings too, and Debbie hums along from her place on the edge of the circle. I sit and lean against a cushion and realise how tired I am.

Show me peace
Amid the roar
Show me peace, show me peace
Find me waves
Along the shore
Show me peace, show me peace
Blow across the open sky

Show me peace before I die
Come for me with gentle song
Speak of good and not of wrong
Show me peace
Among the waves
Show me peace, show me peace
Show me peace
Among the graves
Show me peace, show me peace.

The flames are roaring, the fire high. I feel their warmth sending me to sleep, but I can't because the sound of the drums is vibrating towards us, scores of them, hard and strong. They start slow and steady, but grow more insistent, more powerful, until shouts are rising above the beats and I can't help but feel energised, excited.

There must be at least fifty of them. Native Americans; men, women and children, all in traditional clothing. They fill the tipi, the sound of their drums deafening, primal, overwhelming. There are enormous drums, three or four feet in diameter, with six or more people thundering them at once, smaller drums thumping and clashing, and people singing and dancing. Ric throws himself into the crowd and loses himself to the swell, and before long the others are dancing too; Angharad, Debbie, even Davis is jumping up and down with nervous excitement. It's only Tyrone that isn't dancing; he sits at the edge of the tipi, scowling.

I can almost forget everything, think of nothing. Just exist and be, among the beats, among the rhythms that rise and fall. Debbie dances past and she is alive, just as alive as any of the others. It's almost like that night in the pit never happened. Almost.

Ric bounces towards me, glowing. 'Pablo!' he shouts. 'Let's go!' He grabs my arm and pulls me out of the tipi, runs through the trees, and I follow him. The air is fresh and still after the heat and noise in the tipi and I gulp it down and run, as fast as I can, my heart racing, my lungs burning. It feels good to run again, to be free to run again.

The trees get closer together and Ric slows and stops. Hidden in thick vegetation ahead of us is a small, domed hut constructed out of bent saplings and animal hides.

'Sweat lodge,' Ric beams. He hauls up the entrance flap, beckons me inside and closes the flap. He starts chanting straight away, slow and solemn, and scoops water onto hot boulders in the centre of the hut. The lodge fills with steam and heat, and I sit and feel myself relax, muscle by muscle.

I lose track of time in the heat, the steam, the never ending chanting that echoes deep down the wires, into my brain.

'Debbie?' She is poised on our ledge, above the pit.

'Leave me alone.'

'Please, Debbie.'

'Please what?' She lifts her head and glares at me. Her eyes are red and sore and her face is hard with anger and pain. I hate it when she's like this.

'Come home.'

'Why? Why should I? To make you feel better?'

'Just come home, please, I'll protect you.'

'No you won't, you never do.' She looks down at the pit.

'I will. This time I will.'

'*NO, YOU WON'T*. You can't stop him. You are weak. You are a coward.' She pushes me away and I stumble backwards, and she moves in closer and punches me hard on the jaw. 'You can't stop him. You won't. You don't care.'

'I do care, Debbie. Please, come home.'

'*NO*. You can't protect me. You won't protect me.'

'This time I will, I promise.' My eyes are stinging and I blink fast.

'I don't believe you. You're a liar. A liar and a coward.' She punches me again. 'You're stupid. You don't understand. You're weak and you're a coward.' She hits me, again and again. 'You listen and you watch and you do nothing.' She hits me, and hits me, and I let her, I let her hit me. I deserve it. 'You're as bad as him. Worse. You know it's

177

wrong but you let it happen. You're a coward.' She hits me on the chin, and on the temple. She hits and hits and it hurts. It really hurts. There is blood and swelling and throbbing and pain and all of a sudden it has to stop. *IT HAS TO STOP*, but she isn't listening. She's screaming at me, and I can't see for the blood, and this has to stop, so I push her away.

And she falls.

Into the pit.

I look over the edge and see her, far below, still, her face frozen in a silent scream, her eyes glazed. Water surrounds her face and her hair floats up and the wind blows around my face. And she sings.

Oh happy day
Oh happy day
Oh happy day
Oh happy day
When he washed
When he washed
He washed my sins away
Oh happy day.

I stagger out of the sweat lodge and throw up.

There are no second chances.

I crouch, hunched over, trying to spit the taste of bile from my mouth. Dark, faceless figures move through the black air; Native American men are filing into the sweat lodge. Some of them stop and ask if I am all right, and I nod a lie.

Ric springs down beside me and slaps my back.

'Debbie wants to talk to you again.'

My stomach clenches. I feel sick again.

'She hasn't finished. You must come back in.' He pulls at my arm and I wrench it back.

'I'm finished in there.'

'No, you're not.' Ric grabs me with both arms and hauls me up, pushes me back towards the lodge, and I think about fighting him off, but I've no fight in me, not anymore.

We sit in the lodge, full of sweaty torsos swaying, a different voice chanting. Ric is smiling. I don't see his face, but you can feel Ric's smile, you can feel it split the air around him.

'It wasn't your fault, Paulie.' Debbie is sitting between two warriors, their heads hanging down.

Yes, it was.

'I was going to jump anyway.'

Maybe. Maybe not. That's not the point.

'OK, so it was your fault. Move on. Everyone has to live with mistakes, regrets.'

Not everyone kills their sister.

'Everyone has problems, Paulie.' Her head rises above a man with long, grey hair. 'This man shot his friend when he was out hunting.' She moves around the drummers. 'This man lost his daughter; he searches for her every day, calling her name. This man's mother died and he will always wish they were closer, always think of things he left unsaid.'

THEY DIDN'T KILL THEIR SISTER.

'*WHOSE LOSS IS WORSE?* Whose pain is greater? You can't compare these things, Paulie. It doesn't matter what happened, it only matters how you deal with it.' She drifts away into the steam, into the sweat, and the chanting goes on and on.

CHAPTER THIRTY

I wake on the floor of a clearing. Dawn is lightening the air to a soft grey. Birds are singing, insects floating aimlessly between the trees. My overalls are soaked with sweat and dew from the grass. I am cold and stiff and my head hurts. A fire is smouldering nearby and I taste ash in the air and on my lips. I can't hear Debbie but I know she is close. I can feel her in the breeze.

Ric is leaning over me, beaming. 'Come on, Pablo, we're leaving.'

'I'm not coming.'

'You are coming.'

'I'm going to the police. I should be serving five years for manslaughter.'

Two years to go. Maybe three. Then I will be free.

Ric waves his hand, like what I just said is

nothing. 'You have to do something first.'

I sit up, and my head spins. Slowly, the world comes into focus. Davis is huddled next to Angharad. Tyrone is sitting away from them, his eyebrows tense and furrowed.

'We're all leaving together.' Ric looks around at everyone. 'We're all going to fight together.' He raises his arms into the air and laughs, like this is all a game, like it's the most fun he's had in years. 'The spirits have spoken. Chief Two Sticks sent me a vision.'

'Go where? Fight who?' Tyrone rises to his feet. 'This is *stupid*!' he shouts. 'You are *CRAZY*. You are *ALL* crazy.'

'What do you want to do, Tyrone?' Angharad asks calmly.

'*I DON'T KNOW!*' Tyrone stares at her, his eyes blazing so much I feel their heat. 'I need my medicines.'

Davis lifts his head, his gaze darting from tree to tree. 'I need my medicines, too. Without them the shadows are worse. They keep shouting for help and I don't know what to do.'

'It can take time to understand the spirits.' Ric crouches next to Davis.

'I want to go back,' Davis says. 'They were helping me get rid of the shadows. I don't want them.'

Angharad picks up Davis' hand and I'm sure I see a spark. 'It's not always a bad thing to hear voices. Sometimes it just takes time to figure out how to talk to them. Sometimes they can help.'

'*I HATE IT,*' Tyrone shouts. A rock cracks open on the floor at his feet, revealing a clean, shiny surface inside. 'I hate it all.' He storms away from us, hovers at the edge of the clearing.

'If we go to the police …' I begin.

'It's the police that sent you there in the first place.' Debbie is sat on a low branch, swinging her legs back and forth.

'What they were doing at Tŷ Hapus can't be legal.' I look at Angharad. 'They wouldn't send us back there.'

Angharad shakes her head. 'I'm not taking that risk. I'm going with Ric, I'm keeping my sisters. I know there is a place for us. I know there are others like us.'

'What place? How do you know?'

'I've been there.'

'For real? In a dream? In a vision?' I feel anger rising. The wind blows between the trees, lifts ash into the air. A helicopter drums overhead and we all back into the woods. Listen to it approach. Listen to it fade away.

Angharad looks at Davis and Tyrone. 'You can go back if you want. Or you can stay with me. I can take you somewhere safe, where you can get the help you need.' She starts walking and Davis stays with her, still gripping her hand, and she glances back at me. 'Come on,' she says.

'Sometimes you have to have faith that things will get better if you keep moving forwards.'

'This is stupid,' Tyrone grumbles, but he steps forwards and follows her.

Ric bounds over to me, beaming. 'Come on, Pablo, time to move on.'

'Yes, come on, Paulie,' Debbie jumps down from her branch. 'The spirits have spoken,' she mimics Ric's rough voice, 'and the good Lord has a plan,' she sings in Pam's powerful tones.

I follow her across the clearing and back into the woods.

What does Angharad mean about a safe place, about others like us?

'I don't know. She's crazy. You're all crazy.'

Shut up.

I smile. Whatever else is going on, it's good to have Debbie with me.

Ric starts chanting and I don't want to hear it again today so I try and talk to him. 'Do you know where Angharad is going, Ric?'

'There is a battle coming, Pablo. The first battle in a war.' Ric's eyes are shining, excited. 'Some people,' he says, 'have spirits so powerful they can't be controlled. That's what will stop them.' He nods to Angharad walking ahead of us. 'She is one of them. You will free her, and she will stop them.'

'She's already free, Ric. Do you know where she's going?'

'To the others, like her. We'll leave her on a beach and they'll find her and I'll return to the spirit world.'

'You'll return to the spirit world?'

'There are so many of them,' Ric lifts his fingers to his temples, 'it's hard sometimes to understand them all.' For a moment he looks strained, tired, then all of a sudden his face breaks and he laughs. He mumbles something and I realise he's laughing at something one of his voices said. 'Some of them are tricksters, you have to be careful who you listen to, and ...' An old man appears at the side of Ric. He has long white hair, and is wearing a top hat and waistcoat. The skin of his bare arms wrinkles out of it in deep folds. '... And sometimes the effort it takes to hide them can make them difficult to hear.' Ric turns to the old man and talks to him for a while. He turns back to me and the man disappears. 'I belong in their world, Pablo. If I was in their world I wouldn't have to hide them. I would hear them clearly.'

'If you were in the spirit world?'

Ric nods.

'Then you'd be dead.'

'Death is just a journey to the spirit world.'

'No it's not,' I grab Ric's arm, 'death is *dead* and *gone*.'

Ric looks at Debbie, skipping along to my right, 'Really?'

'Whether she's in my head, or in your head, or

even if she is a spirit or a ghost, she is still *dead* and *gone*.' I feel anger rising. I look at Debbie and my eyes sting. 'That's not Debbie.'

Debbie had hopes and dreams, a future. I was going to take her away; we were going to make a fresh start and we were going to be free from Dad. She was going to be a singer; I was going to be a boxer.

Now it's just me and a voice in my head.

I look at Ric muttering to his voices. He doesn't understand. He's crazy.

Ric puts his hand on my arm, stops for a moment, and looks me straight in the eye, 'Paul,' he says firmly; he calls me by my name so I know this is serious. 'You have to make sure Angharad is safe. Don't let them pull her to pieces.'

I nod. I will make sure everyone is safe. Tyrone, Davis, Angharad, Ric. This time I will get it right.

'She can't stop him yet, but she will. You have to keep her safe because one day, when she is with the others, she will stop him.'

'Who?'

Ric turns to one of his voices and laughs, starts talking, and I realise I've lost him again.

CHAPTER
THIRTY-ONE

It's dark when we reach the coast. I smell salt on the wind, the earth turns sandy, and the trees thin until there are none at all and we are walking across sand dunes, heading towards a beach and a huge bonfire. The whole day has been a blur of voices and arguments and singing and chanting, and I realise I have completely lost whatever grip I had on reality.

Drums are thundering. Native American dancers thump around the flames, lost in the pounding, bouncing in and out of the haze of smoke. It plumes into the air, gets caught by the wind, and drifts across the black sky, but the stars shine on, shine on through the fog of it.

The ocean, somewhere close but invisible in the dark, creates a steady backbeat of ebb and flow, of sand stirring and pebbles clinking together. I sit on the cool sand and try not to think, neither of the past nor the future, just try to exist in the moment; the smoke, the ocean, the drums.

Ric and Angharad are dancing, together but apart. Davis is tapping his feet nervously and Tyrone is hiding behind his eyebrows at the edge of the group. Anger radiates from him like the fire, and as he stares at it, flaming branches bend and crack.

'Dance with me, Paulie,' Debbie smiles. I don't remember her ever looking so joyful.

No.

I am sorry. I wish I could jump up and dance, show some joy, like her. I am sort of joyful. More joyful than I have been in ... forever. I am free. Debbie is with me. I have escaped Tŷ Hapus, and got the others out too. Even though I've no idea where we are going, it's better than knowing tomorrow I will wake up in Tŷ Hapus, or back at home with Dad.

Debbie wanders off and dances around the fire with the others. I walk over to Tyrone, and sit next to him.

'Tyrone.'

He scowls an acknowledgment.

'You all right?'

'*NO*!' He shouts; his face full of pain.

I hear his voices. They are angry, desperate, helpless.

Get off me. Leave me alone. Go away.

'Your voices are angry.' It's a stupid thing to say.

Tyrone grimaces at the fire.

I am lost.

Debbie? How can I help him?

'You can't.' Debbie sits next to me. 'You can't help everyone.'

But I took him out of Tŷ Hapus. I am responsible for him. Who else does he have?

'My voices *are* angry,' Tyrone turns to me, 'and *I CAN'T TAKE IT ANYMORE*. At least in Tŷ Hapus they would give me medicines and they would go away for a while. Now they are here all the time, and they *SHOUT* and they *SCREAM*, and they are getting louder, and there is the man, *LOOK*.' Tyrone points at the fire. 'That man is always here, always watching, always following me and I know he is going to *KILL ME*, he is going to *KILL US ALL*.' Tyrone looks to the ocean, invisible behind the night. 'There are eyes out there, do you see them, glowing red in the dark?'

I look at the fire, towards the ocean, and I see nothing.

'You don't believe me.'

'Of course I believe you.' I point at Debbie. 'Do you see my sister? She's sitting next to me, humming her favourite song.'

Tyrone shakes his head.

'Well, I do, and to me she is real. As real as

189

when she was alive. Just because you don't see her doesn't make her any less real.'

Tyrone's eyebrows relax a tiny fraction.

'Just because we see things other people don't, doesn't mean they aren't there. That's what I think, anyway.'

'But you like seeing your sister.'

I nod.

'Well, I *HATE* that man, and the eyes, and the angry voices. *EVERYTHING* I see is angry and it threatens me and I don't want this anymore.'

I don't know what to say, what to do.

'Take me back. To Tŷ Hapus.'

'But what they do is wrong, Tyrone. The tests, the drugs, the wires.'

Tyrone frowns again, a deep, pained frown. 'But they can get rid of the voices. That's what they were trying to do.'

I look at the fire. 'If you still want to go back tomorrow, I'll take you to another hospital, a different one. There has to be a better way to help you, without the wires and the drugs. If you saw what they did to Saeed –'

Tyrone stands and walks away to the other side of the fire.

Debbie looks over at him. 'He was abandoned, neglected, abused. His foster father –'

I don't want to know.

'Davis watched his family burn. Angharad lost two sisters. They were swimming in the sea. She

190

tried to save them but a current carried them away.'

I GET IT. I DON'T WANT TO KNOW.

Their pain just adds to mine, pain on pain, it doesn't help.

'You can all move on.' Debbie stands and looks towards the black ocean.

'*AYAYAYAYAYAYAY*,' Ric's voice rises high above the beats, and is joined by whoops and yelps from the drummers.

'Ric has a loving family the other side of the world. He left them.'

What? Why?

'Something as simple as a broken heart can break you, Paulie, if you let it.'

How do you know all this? You told me you're in my head.

'I could be. All of this could be in your head.'

A drumming bears down from above, and I realise what it is just as the light hits the dancers, stops them mid bound, and makes them shield their eyes. The light swings away and one of the drummers shouts, and Ric, Angharad and Davis start running towards the dunes.

I can't see Tyrone. I hear the whir of the helicopter, the pounding of the blades; it has landed somewhere on the beach, not far away, in the darkness. Sand is swirling through the smoke, and I can't see Tyrone. My eyes dart around, stinging from the sand, but I can't find him. I skirt through the darkness enclosing the fire. I have to find him. I can't let them take him away.

'He wanted to leave, Paulie. He wanted to go back.' Debbie bounces around in front of me, her hair blowing in the wind.

That's not the point.

'It *IS* the point. Let him go. You have to run, Paulie, now.'

I can't let them take him. I took him out of Tŷ Hapus. I'm responsible for him.

I think about Saeed and I know I have to get him back.

'Are there *ANY* smarts in there?' Debbie throws a punch and I duck out of the way. I keep moving towards the noise of the helicopter blades whirring.

'Paul, this is stupid. They are going to catch you, and then they are going to get rid of me.'

A metallic creak echoes through the darkness ahead and I sprint towards the noise. The outline of the helicopter emerges from the darkness, and Tyrone, small beside it, bending it. I run to him as fast as I can.

The hard-faced man steps out of the helicopter, strides towards Tyrone, and the creaking stops, the bending stops, and Tyrone falls to the floor, and I run faster. The sand pulls each of my steps back and I run faster and faster, but Tyrone is down, and the man has picked him up and is carrying him into the helicopter, and I run but I know I won't make it. The wind roars ahead of me, blasting a sandstorm towards the man, but he is already stepping into the helicopter. I see a symbol on its door; yellow concentric circles, like a target, like Ric's tattoo, and for a moment I wonder if it is even real.

Two black uniforms step out of the helicopter. Lightning sheets flash across the sky, and a dazzling fork smacks down onto the sand. I turn away from it and see Angharad behind me. Then a uniform runs towards me and a scream fills my head, a scream so loud I fall to the floor and clutch my head to keep it from bursting open. I turn to Angharad. It takes a while to work my gaze through the scream, and when I do I see she is on the floor too, cradling her own head.

Anger surges inside me and a cyclone smashes out and up into the sky, but there is a uniform standing over me, his hair and clothes flapping in the wind but his body solid, and he stabs something into my arm and blackness crashes down. My last thought is about Debbie, about how she is right, about how I'm not known for my smarts.

CHAPTER
THIRTY-TWO

There is a picture buried in the black sand. I reach down and pick it up, dust the sand off. I recognise it from years ago. It was on the mantelpiece in the old house. The bungalow. Where Mum died.

It's a photograph of a couple with the sea behind them. They are smiling, holding each other tight, the surface of the water shining behind them. The photograph is black and white, but it always looked more colourful than anything else in that house.

I was maybe three or four when I asked Debbie who the couple in the photograph were. She said they were Mum and Dad. For years after that I thought we were adopted. That the happy couple in the photograph were our real parents, and the people we lived with were our other parents, our adoptive ones, like the step parents out of fairy tales. The mum we lived with was always sad and praying. The dad was always drunk and angry. They looked nothing like our real parents; the couple in the photograph.

I used to daydream that our real parents would come and get us one day, and take us to the shining sea in the photograph. Sometimes I would imagine it was a beach with golden sand. We would build sandcastles and splash in the rolling waves for hours. Sometimes I would imagine a harbour full of boats, the smell of fish and chips on the wind, and a lighthouse in the distance. And sometimes I would imagine we were all on a boat, sailing away.

When Mum died they put the picture next to her coffin and I realised no one was coming to take us away.

CHAPTER THIRTY-THREE

My mouth is dry, cracked. I know something is wrong as soon as I wake. I feel like I have been asleep for a hundred years, and I can't feel Debbie. I can't feel her at all. My head is cold, numb, bandaged tight. Someone shines a light into one eye, then the other. It pierces like a needle. My stomach lurches with the realisation that I have been here before.

'What is your name?'

I know that voice. I open my eyes and everything is metal, dull, grey metal; the ceiling, the walls. I try to move, but there are restraints; they feel cold and hard.

'What is your name?'

'Paul,' I croak. 'Paul Ogaji.'

'Do you remember me, Paul? Dr Epstein. It's

nice to see you again; I've been worried about you.'

'Angharad –'

'She's fine,' Dr Epstein smiles, 'and so are Tyrone, Davis and Ric.'

My heart sinks to the back of my chest. They have them all.

'You have been here, in Tŷ Eidolon, for just over a week now.'

A week. I feel suffocated. I gasp for air.

'We have removed your intracranial monitors, Paul. How are you feeling?'

I stare at him, hard. I want to punch the smile from his face. This time I will. I will do it before I leave.

'Can you move your fingers?'

I clench my fists.

Dr Epstein pulls his chair closer. 'We have done extensive tests this last week, and we are now confident we can completely cure your condition. It would be a simple operation, and the results would be permanent. You would not require any further medications, and you could leave here and start a new life.'

'I don't want to be cured,' I growl through clenched teeth. They are not cutting into my brain. They are not taking Debbie.

'I thought as much,' Dr Epstein smiles. 'You are very attached to your sister, aren't you, Paul?'

I stare at him, anger rising. Where is the wind?

Where is Debbie?

'There is another option, Paul.' Dr Epstein leans back in his chair and clicks his pen. 'Would you like to hear about it?'

I don't want to listen to anything he has to say. I just want to get out of here.

'We could control your condition with medications instead; continue as we started in Tŷ Hapus. It is a less permanent solution, but it has its benefits.' Dr Epstein clicks his pen again. 'You would be able to see your sister, sometimes. But you would be more in control. We could switch her off, so to speak, like we have now. I'm sure you can see the benefits of that.'

'I don't want medication. I am fine.'

'I'm afraid that's not an option, Paul. You are not fine. You have highly irregular brain activity and it needs to be controlled. If we don't treat you, it will get worse. You are already a danger to yourself, and to others. But we can help you.' He leans forwards, adds weight to his voice. 'We can help you control what you can do, maybe even make it useful.'

I think I understand what he is saying now. 'You want me to be useful. You want to turn me into a weapon? A soldier?'

Dr Epstein leans back and laughs. It is a dry, hollow sound. 'No, Paul, not at all. We just want to help you control your condition. To keep you, and others around you, safe.' He lowers his voice,

'However, if it emerges that you have useful skills, then of course there is the possibility that you might choose to use them in a suitable vocation, and perhaps we can help you with that.' He stands and puts his pen in his pocket. 'But we can talk about that later. So, do I take it you are prepared to continue with the medication?'

I stare at him and nod slightly. It is the only choice that leaves me with a chance of getting out of here with Debbie, and the others.

'Where are the others?'

'Tyrone and Davis are doing very well. They're staying in a dormitory with boys like them, and are settling in well. Their conditions are under control and they are learning to use their talents productively. I hope you will join them soon.' Dr Epstein smiles and looks at me like he thinks I might smile back.

'What about Angharad and Ric?'

'They are fine, undergoing assessment.' Dr Epstein walks away. A door opens and shuts heavily behind him.

It is only when he is gone I realise there is a uniform in the room with me.

'Hello, Paul,' he smiles, like we're going to be best friends. 'I'm going to remove your restraints now.' I'm not sure what he does but the cold restraints around my arms and legs seem to disappear. 'You can sit up now, but take your time.'

I don't have any choice but to take my time. My body is slow, weak. I notice I am wearing a black overall, like him. He is big, muscled, but he can't be that much older than me.

'I'm Victor,' he smiles again. 'Dr Epstein said if you're feeling up to it I can take you on a short tour. Would you like something to eat first?'

I nod and Victor leaves. The whole room is metal, floor to ceiling. I rise slowly and stare at the sky out of the window until the spinning stops, then walk to the glass, my bare feet recoiling from the cold floor.

A large open quad is below me; the building is a square around it, and I must be on the first floor. A few black uniforms are down in the quad. I don't know if they are guards, or inmates, or patients. Three of them are large; they could be guards. But four others are much smaller, and look younger. All of them seem to be playing a game together. Oversized metal bowling pins are scattered across the quad, some standing, some fallen; they have colours and numbers on their necks.

The door opens. 'Food.' Victor pushes a chair closer to the window and nods to it. I sit and take the tray. 'It's a simple game.' Victor looks out of the window. 'You knock down pins for points.'

I scoop soup into my mouth and stare out of the window. One of the pins falls, and the uniforms clap and cheer.

'How?' I ask.

'With your voices; your powers. I'll take you down to try if you like.'

I scoop more soup.

'It's good training.'

'For what?'

Victor smiles. 'You know, just to learn how to control them. To see what they can do. How many voices do you have?'

'One.'

'Me too.' Victors nods to the uniforms down in the quad. 'Some of them have lots of voices.'

'How many patients are here?'

'Trainees. About twenty.'

'How many guards?'

Victor laughs. 'There are no guards. We're all here because we want to be here.'

I don't believe him. 'You want to be here?'

Victor nods. 'Tŷ Eidolon is a special place for special people. None of us would want to be anywhere else.'

'But the doctors, the tests, the drugs …' I don't believe him. Not everyone wants to be here.

'I know it can be difficult, but it is all designed to help, and the worst is over; Dr Epstein says he has established what medications you need. It's not like Tŷ Hapus, it's all about testing there, but here it's all about training. It's fun. Come on.' He lifts a pair of shoes from under the table I was lying on. 'I'll show you around and you can see for yourself.'

I put on the shoes and follow Victor along a wide metal corridor. He nods to the doors on either side. 'These are all private rooms; you shouldn't be up here long. The dormitories are on the floor below us.'

Private rooms. Isolation rooms. They have locks. Not everyone wants to be here.

We pass through a set of doors, go down a staircase and continue along an identical metal corridor. 'The training rooms are along here.'

'Training rooms?'

Victor opens the nearest door and I follow him into an enormous hall. A massive slab of formless metal sits in the middle of the space.

'You know Tyrone,' Victor points to a group of three uniforms sitting in front of the metal. Tyrone stands and looks at me; no frowns or scowls or grimaces, he just looks at me, calm. The wires are missing from his head, his scars freshly stitched.

'Tyrone, are you all right?'

He nods, and the corners of his mouth twitch upwards. 'Watch this, Paul.' He stares at the metal and it slowly bends, moulds, like giant invisible thumbs are squashing it. Slowly, it takes the shape of a tipi, Ric's tipi, complete with the pictures on its cover engraved into the metal.

'That's amazing, Tyrone.' It really is.

Tyrone smiles proudly.

'Good work,' Victor nods. 'Keep practising. You can catch up with Paul later.'

Tyrone sits and Victor leads me out, further along the corridor. 'The canteen is down that corridor,' he points around a corner, 'or I could take you out to the quad and show you the game.'

I nod and follow Victor through some double doors into the quad. No locks. I wonder if it is true that everyone wants to be here. It can't be.

Faces turn to look at us as we approach. There are seven uniforms, all children, although some are much older than others.

'Carry on,' Victor nods.

'It's your turn, Wasim,' a small, white-haired boy shouts.

There is a rush of movement and air, and one of the metal pins falls to the floor. 'Six points,' a tall, skinny boy says breathlessly.

'No, I saw you move.' The white-haired boy waves an arm in the direction of the pin. A couple of the others nod agreement.

'No way,' Wasim shakes his head. 'I was faster than that.'

'I saw you,' Victor smiles. 'You're not as fast as you think.'

'Three points?' Wasim raises his eyebrows.

The white-haired boy ignores him. 'Hasan, your turn,' he says to a boy with burn scars on his cheeks.

Hasan flicks his wrist and a fireball shoots across the quad, knocks down one of the pins, and disappears into the air.

'Eight points. Bethan.'

One of the pins floats up into the air, higher and higher, until it is hovering above the building, then it smashes to the floor with a metallic clang.

'That's just showing off,' Wasim shakes his head.

'Would you like a turn?' Victor points at a pin in the far corner of the quad. 'Knock that one down. Just that one.'

I shake my head.

'Oh yeah, sorry, hold on,' Victor pulls three syringes out of his breast pocket. Two are red and one is green; I notice they have my name on. 'May I?' Victor lifts the green syringe.

'What?'

'It will bring your voice back.'

I hold out my hand. I want to see Debbie.

Victor injects cold into the back of my hand, and I feel like I have jumped into icy water. I feel so alive, so awake, and there is Debbie, in front of me, floating, like she did in the pit. My breath catches in my throat.

Debbie?

'I'm here, Paulie,' she whispers. She is faint, her eyes are cloudy. It's Debbie, but it's not Debbie, it's like the ghost of her ghost.

What have they done to her? Anger wells inside me and the wind rises.

'Try and focus it,' Victor shouts over the wind. 'Knock that pin over.'

Debbie?

'I'm here, Paulie,' she whispers. She doesn't sound right; she's weak.

Spar with me, Debbie.

'I'm here, Paul.'

She's not here. It's an illusion. Pain and anger ache in my chest. The wind swirls around the quad, all the pins wobble, and one of them falls over. I hear the others laughing.

Victor points at the pin in the corner. 'That one,' he shouts, 'focus on that one.'

I stare at Victor and my anger rises, the wind rises. This is all stupid; a stupid pointless game. They have taken Debbie, they have taken Angharad, and they have taken Ric, and I don't trust them. I don't trust any of them. Wind surges around the quad and all the pins smash to the floor and skid across the concrete. I look for the nearest door, for a way out. I start to run but the floor seems to tilt and I fall to my knees, and as I am trying to get up I feel a needle pierce my neck and the wind suddenly stops, and Debbie is gone.

CHAPTER
THIRTY-FOUR

The picture, the one from the mantelpiece in the old house, the bungalow, is next to the coffin and the realisation that the smiling face in the photograph once belonged to my sad, dead mother is slowly dawning on me.

Music is droning, a dirge of notes that oppresses the congregation into silence. Their faces are hard and stiff. Maybe they are holding themselves tense and solid to try and stop the emotions from seeping out and overwhelming them. If I look closely at the little details, I can see them trickling through the cracks; I see them in the flaring nostrils; the blinking eyes; the mouths held in thin, tight lines; the trembling hands.

The music stops and a priest stands and starts talking, but I don't listen. I look at my father. His head is hung low and I don't recognise his expression. He isn't angry. Maybe he is sad. He is clutching a hymn book tightly. Maybe he is sad and angry at the same time. He is so tall, everyone is so tall. I feel trapped. The air is crushing me; it is so still and heavy.

I step away from my father and he doesn't notice. I tiptoe to the wall, skirt it all the way to the back of the church, and slip out of the door into the fresh air. My heart is racing. I know I am doing something wrong. I should be in there, in the oppressive church, with my sad, dead mother in the box and those stiff faces full of emotion. I am doing something wrong but I can't help myself. I want to be in the warmth and the light and I want to see the sky and feel the breeze on my skin.

I start running. It feels good to run. I weave between the gravestones, jump across their shadows. They are huge, taller than me, towering slabs with names carved into them, lifetimes summed up in a few words. My shoes are too small; they hurt my feet, so I take them off and sprint barefoot across the graves. I know I am doing something wrong but I can't help myself. I look at the flowers and the sky and the clouds and I feel almost happy in this stolen moment. I know I will pay for this later but I can't help myself.

A man is at the gate, a tall man with a hard face and a painful stare. He is wearing a black uniform and he doesn't belong here, he isn't part of this memory. He doesn't open his mouth but he speaks to me with a strong voice; the sort of voice you don't argue with.

'You don't need to go back in. You can come with me.'

I look at him and I know he is all kinds of wrong. I am not meant to be with him, but he is stood at the gate in the sunshine and the warmth and all of a sudden the graveyard is cold and grey and the church behind me is icy and black and holds nothing more than my dead mother and my sad, angry father and the confusing emotion-filled faces. And Debbie. *I can't leave Debbie.*

The sky darkens even more and the wind sweeps between the gravestones and billows the robes of the choir gathered around her grave. Debbie's grave. Her coffin is lowered into the ground. I am stood next to a policeman and a priest is talking but I don't hear his words.

'There is nothing left here. You can come with me.' The man opens the gate and I turn to him. He is in the sunshine and the warmth; flowers are growing around his feet, and although I know it is wrong, I step forwards and walk out of the gate. I know it is wrong but I can't help myself. I do it anyway.

CHAPTER
THIRTY-FIVE

I wake on a hard table. There is a bright light right above my face and I can't move: restraints are pinning me down.

'I am still confident his activity is controllable with the medications.' Dr Epstein's voice is behind me. He is unclipping wires from a cap on my head.

'He doesn't want the medications. He'll keep fighting.' A strong voice; the sort of voice you don't argue with.

'Shall I schedule the operation, then?' Dr Epstein asks.

'Victor?' The strong voice again.

'Today was my fault; I shouldn't have given him the injection so soon. It confused him. I think it's worth giving him another chance. I'd be happy to guide his training.'

'He's awake.' Dr Epstein pulls off the cap.

The light flicks off and the restraints slide away.

'Sit up, Paul.' The strong voice.

I sit up. The voice belongs to the hard-faced man. He stares at me and I feel a sharp pain in the centre of my forehead. He looks away and the pain disappears. 'One week.' He nods to Victor, and strides out of the room.

'Who is he?' I ask Victor.

'The director.'

'The director?'

'Of Eventual Eidolon.' Victor taps the logo on his sleeve, and my sleeve. Yellow concentric circles, like on the helicopter, like Ric's tattoo. 'It's what we're all a part of. The director finds those with powers and helps them develop their skills so they can use them productively.'

Dr Epstein steps into view. 'Paul, this is an opportunity for you to be part of something truly great. If you choose to stay here you will be with people like yourself. You will have a home, a family, and you will be with your sister.' He smiles the sympathetic smile I hate. 'You will be trained, and ultimately given a purpose in life.'

'And if I choose not to stay you will cut some of my brain off.'

'That's a little melodramatic, Paul. It is a simple procedure that would enable you to lead a normal life in the outside world.' Dr Epstein picks up a folder of notes. 'We cannot release you as you are.

It's simply not safe.' Dr Epstein turns to Victor. 'Why don't you put him in a dorm with Tyrone and Davis? It might help him to see how much they've progressed in such a short space of time.' Dr Epstein walks towards the door. 'The director said you have a week, Paul. I hope you are still here at the end of it. You and your sister.'

Victor smiles, 'You'll like it here, Paul, if you give it a chance.'

'Where are Angharad and Ric?'

'I'm sure they will join you in time. Come on, I'll show you to your dorm.' Victor leads me into a cold, metal corridor.

'What's with all the metal?'

'It's just safer. There are a few fire generators here. It's easier to clean, too; some of the powers can get messy.'

'Everyone here has some kind of power?'

Victor smiles. 'Cool, isn't it?'

'I don't know. What do you do with your powers?'

'Train, mostly. Sometimes we go on missions to find others.'

'But why? What does the director want with you all?'

'He wants to give us a safe home and help us develop our skills.'

'But he must want something in return.'

Victor opens a door and I follow him down a flight of stairs. 'The dormitories are along here.'

He opens a door and beckons me inside. There are six beds arranged neatly, three on either side of the room. Victor points to one in a back corner. 'You can have that one. The others will return from training soon and you can catch up with Tyrone and Davis before dinner.'

I sit on the bed and look at the door. It doesn't have a lock.

'It's good here, Paul. Honestly.' Victor looks sincere. 'The drug tests are finished. It's all about training now. People like us; we can be superheroes,' he smiles, 'for real.'

'Or supervillains,' I mutter.

Victor laughs, 'I guess it depends how you look at it.'

'Everyone is controlled with drugs.'

'It's not like that,' Victor shakes his head, 'we're all in control of our own treatment.'

'My voice isn't the same. When you injected me before and my voice came, it wasn't the same.'

Victor shakes his head. 'It won't be. That's the way the drugs work. You'll get used to it. It's better: safer, more controlled.'

I stare at the door. I want to say it's not better. I don't want to control Debbie. I just want to see her, as she is, as she was, in life.

Voices drift down the corridor towards us.

'Here are the trainees,' Victor smiles as boys file into the dorm, all in black overalls with the yellow logo.

'You know Davis and Tyrone. That's Eli,' he points to the white-haired boy I saw in the quad, 'and that's Aiden,' he points to an older boy with long, brown hair. 'This is Paul,' he shouts over the boys' conversations. 'He'll be staying in here.'

The boys nod greetings. Davis jogs over and looks at me without scanning the room, without twitching, without being distracted by his shadows. 'Hi, Paul. Are you all right?'

I nod a lie. 'Hi, Davis. How are you getting on?'

Davis sits and shuffles back on the bed. 'It's good here, Paul.' He pulls three syringes out of his breast pocket, two red and one green; they all have his name on them. 'This one,' Davis holds up a green syringe, 'brings the shadows, but different to before,' he smiles. 'They listen to me, they do what I want,' he holds up the red syringe, 'and this one stops the shadows,' he puts the syringes back in his pocket and taps it gently, 'and I have them, Paul, I decide when to use them. It's not like in Tŷ Hapus. They trust us here, they help us.'

'Do they give you other medicines?' I ask.

'We get pills or injections in the morning,' Davis nods, 'to keep the voices away until we want to bring them.'

I look around the dorm. Tyrone is laughing with Eli, Victor is chatting to Aiden. They look happy, relaxed. Davis is right; it's not like Tŷ Hapus. It doesn't feel right, but part of me is drawn to it. I have that feeling that I know it is wrong, but I can't

215

help myself.

Davis leans closer to me. 'You know the shadows, Paul? My shadows?'

I nod.

'They do things for me, now. I control them.'

'Like what?' I ask.

'I can send them places and they tell me what they see.'

I wonder how that would be useful for anything other than spying.

'What can the other boys do?' I ask.

Davis points to Aiden. 'He can make fire, and Eli makes fog, all different colours.'

'What about Victor?'

'His voices control water,' Davis smiles. 'He can make rain and snow and ice. There are people here that can do all kinds of things,' Davis goes on. 'There's a boy who can make this noise in your head, this scream –'

'I think I met him at the beach.' I remember the pain in my head, clutching it because it felt like it was going to burst open.

'There is a girl who can show you her voices, you know, like they are real people.'

I think about Ric, his illusions.

Tyrone sits down next to us. 'Have you told him what the director can do?'

Davis shakes his head.

'He can read minds,' Tyrone says. 'Well, not everyone's, but a lot of people, and he can do other stuff, he can –'

'Time for dinner,' Victor shouts and the boys file out of the room.

CHAPTER THIRTY-SIX

Everything in the canteen is dull, grey metal, like the rest of the building, and the uniforms sitting at the tables are all black, but the room is full of life and colour. There's smiling and laughing, and I feel warmth and happiness radiating from the faces in the room. I try and push it away, because I know it has to be an illusion. I want to stay angry so I can get out of here, but there is this lingering feeling that part of me wants it.

Victor leads me to a long hatch in the wall and a uniform behind it, an older boy with dark spiky hair, passes us trays of food. Behind him I can see into the kitchen. Hasan, the boy who threw a fireball in the quad, is heating up pans with blue flames that flow from his hands. Salads are floating in the air behind him; lettuce leaves and tiny

219

tomatoes circle around a girl with short, dark hair and come in to land on plates in front of her.

'That's Bethan,' Victor nods at the girl and she smiles. 'Hasan and Hugh,' he points to the other two boys. 'We all take turns in the kitchen. Once you've settled in we'll put you on the rota.'

'Paul!' One of the uniforms sat at a table jumps up and runs towards me. She has long, dark hair and a pretty face. Madeline smiles and grabs my arm. 'Come and sit with me.' She pulls me to her table and introduces me to a sea of faces. 'Agatha,' she points to a thick set girl opposite us, 'Wasim,' the tall, skinny boy from the quad, the fast one, 'Ivy', a slight girl with short curly hair, 'Max,' the boy with the scream. She names a few more, but I sit down and don't look at them. I remind myself that I want to get out of here; that I don't want to make friends. Madeline sits next to me and leans close to my ear. 'How are you, Paul?'

'Fine,' I nod a lie.

'Have you just arrived?'

'Pretty much.'

'It's amazing here, Paul.'

'So I keep hearing.'

'Everyone has these incredible powers, and I was right, you know, it's nothing to do with spirits or ghosts, it's the power of our minds.'

'How do you know?'

'She doesn't.' The thick set girl, Agatha, leans over the table to us. 'We all have different theories;

that we're controlling ghosts, channelling supernatural forces, or we've evolved beyond other humans. No one really knows, though. I don't even think the director knows.'

'He does,' a small boy with big ears nods from the end of the table. 'I've heard him talking with Dr Epstein about it.'

'I can fly,' Madeline beams.

'Levitate,' Agatha corrects.

'I'm getting higher every time. I think I'll be able to fly soon.'

'What can you do?' Agatha looks at me and puts a tomato in her mouth.

'He's an elemental.' Madeline shuffles closer to me and Victor sits down next to her. He passes me a drink and I nod a thank you.

'What's an elemental?' I ask.

'Fire, water, earth, air,' Victor smiles. 'Some of them like to group the powers we have. Elementals, paranormals, physicals –'

'We're physicals,' Madeline waves her hand around the table. 'We have enhanced physical powers. Agatha is super strong, and I can fly.'

'Levitate,' Agatha corrects again. She points at the others. 'Wasim is fast, Ivy can wall crawl, Max has a sonic scream, Josh has enhanced hearing, and Hugh, in the kitchen, can regenerate.'

'The paranormals are mostly over there,' Madeline nods to the table on the far side of the room and frowns.

'What can they do?'

Agatha scans their faces. 'Akim is telekinetic, like Bethan, Didi is clairvoyant, Carla and Davis can astral project, and are training to bilocate, Zhana phase shifts, Poppy creates illusions –'

'There is a boy that can teleport too, where is he?' Madeline looks around.

Agatha laughs. 'Who knows. He could be anywhere!'

'The paranormals have some strange ideas,' Madeline shakes her head. 'Most of them believe in ghosts. They think they have a connection to the spirit world.'

'Their voices tend to be louder,' Victor explains. 'They can be harder to control.'

'There is nothing strange about believing in ghosts,' Ivy looks over to Madeline. 'Nearly everyone in this place hears the voices of people they knew who died. They might well be ghosts; they might well have a connection to the spirit world.'

'I think that emotional trauma might be the driving force that makes the mind develop,' Madeline begins, and I can sense that she is about to launch into her own scientific explanation for it all. 'And then maybe we invent the voices to help explain the powers.'

'Give it a rest, Madeline.' The boy with the big ears puts his fork down, stands up and walks away. 'You talk too much.'

'Just because your ears are oversensitive doesn't mean I have to talk less,' Madeline snaps.

'My ears aren't oversensitive and I think you should talk less,' the boy with the scream, Max looks over to Madeline with cold, deriding eyes.

'It doesn't matter why we are like this,' Victor smiles, clearly trying to break the tension in the air. 'We just are.'

Victor's words fall heavy on my mind. It does matter, because if Debbie isn't a ghost, if she is all in my head, then she is gone, forever.

'Paul ... Paul.'

I look up. Victor is talking to me.

'Are you finished?'

I look at my plate and nod.

'Come on, I'll take you to one of the training rooms.'

I rise to my feet, follow Victor out of the canteen, along a corridor and into a huge, empty hall. He walks to a large metal box in the corner, opens the lid, pulls a spade out of it, and starts shovelling black sand onto the floor.

'What are you doing?'

'Sand has lots of uses in elemental training. It puts out fires, absorbs water. Sasha manipulates it –'

'Sasha?'

'She's an earth mover.'

A huge mound of sand is now on the floor. Victor puts the spade back in the box, passes me a pair of goggles and puts a pair on himself. 'Right. Go on. Move the sand.'

I stare at Victor.

'Oh yeah, sorry,' Victor pulls some syringes out of his pocket and flicks through them until he finds a green one with my name on.

'When do I get to keep my own medicines?'

'The director has to approve. Not long, I'm sure.'

My heart sinks. If he can read minds, like Tyrone said, then I may never get to be in control. I hold out my hand; Victor slides the needle into my skin and the icy sensation flows up my arm and into my body.

Debbie appears in front of me, faint, floating. She is undefined, uncertain, and what I can see of her face looks vacant, devoid of anything but a vague sadness and an aching desire to just be.

Debbie?

She doesn't respond and my eyes sting. I blink fast, and as the tears sink back into my head, anger surges through my chest and the wind rises. Black sand flows from the mound, streams into the air, and moves in great circles around the room.

'Try and control it,' Victor shouts. 'Try to make a shape. A sphere in the middle of the room.'

DEBBIE! I call to her with every fibre of my being but she just floats there, a lifeless imprint of herself like an ancient faded photograph.

The   sand   hurtles   around   the   room

224

uncontrollably, in a million different directions. It smashes into my face, stings my skin until it feels raw.

Victor leans closer to me. 'Just think about a sphere. That's all you have to do. Forget the rest.'

I try not to think about what they have done to Debbie. I will get her back; they can't take her away. I imagine a sphere in the middle of the room. I picture it in my mind and the sand swirls closer and tighter until it is spinning round and round, in the shape of a perfect sphere. It reminds me of the ball of clay in Angharad's hands when we were on the ward in Tŷ Hapus. She pressed the shape of the continents into it.

Continents rise on my sphere of sand. Mountains and valleys form. Rivers flow, ocean currents swirl. The wind gets faster and my world of sand changes; volcanoes explode, plumes of smoke rise to join clouds that drift across the land. Cyclones grow and die over the ocean and my planet made of sand evolves and I get lost in it.

I think about nothing but my planet. I don't know how long I am there before I feel a needle in my neck and the sand stops, and everything falls. My world falls down, and there is just sand on the floor.

CHAPTER THIRTY-SEVEN

Days pass in a blur of training and sleeping. I ask about Angharad and Ric but none of the trainees know where they are and I don't see the doctors. I ask Davis to send his shadows to look for them but he always changes the subject and walks away.

Everything starts to taste sour. I hate myself for not trying to escape. I hate myself for the thoughts I'm having. They don't even feel like my thoughts; that I want to stay even though I know it is wrong; that Debbie is dead and I have to move on; that Ric and Angharad don't matter; that this place will be good for me; that I can be safe and learn to control my powers and be someone useful.

Victor opens the training room door and I follow him in. There are hundreds of plastic balls scattered across the floor.

'What –'

'The director suggested you work on something different today,' Victor smiles. 'He thinks you can burst these balls by expanding the air inside them.'

I hold out my hand for the injection, and a sour taste fills my mouth. The balls roll across the floor, stream down to the far end of the room, pass right through Debbie's lifeless body in the corner, and then the anger comes.

The balls flow back towards me and swirl around my feet and one of them lifts into the air, carried upwards by a tiny whirlwind growing from the floor. I stare at the ball, spinning on the swirling air in front of me, and I think of the air inside it, warming, expanding; the molecules pushing away from each other. The ball cracks and a small gust of stale, warm air puffs out of it; the wind throws the ball against the wall and another one rises into the air in front of me and I stare at it until it cracks.

Time after time I make little vortexes that whirl the balls up and I expand the air inside them until they crack open and then I fling them against the wall. It makes me feel better. It is a release of anger, pain and frustration. Like Debbie used to do when she would hit me, and I would let her.

When there are only a few balls left Victor leans close to me and says, 'Make this one explode,' and I look at it hard. I imagine the air inside it bursting outwards in a rush and the ball suddenly shatters and fragments of sharp plastic fly through the air.

'Good work,' Victor nods.

'Why?' The remaining balls roll to a stop.

'Why what?'

'Why does the director want me to burst balls, make shapes out of sand in the air, make streams and ripples of wind? What's the point of it all?' The sour taste fills my mouth. I'm not in control.

'To see what you can do. To help you realise your potential. We all have so much more power than we realise; all of us here have learned to develop our powers beyond what we ever could have imagined.' Victor picks up one of the last intact balls and it starts raining, a fine misty rain. 'When I first came here I could only make it rain.' The ball in his hand crusts over with ice and the rain turns to snow. The ice thickens and the ball cracks and he drops it to the floor and picks up another. The snow gets heavier and the ball in Victor's hand grows into a huge snowball and he throws it against the wall, picks up the last intact ball and smiles. Ice crystals grow on the ball, becoming more intricate as they rise into the air until it is like a giant snowflake, delicate and symmetrical. He places the sculpture in my hand and it starts to melt. 'Come on,' he says, 'there's one more thing to try today.'

I follow Victor into another training room, the one with the metal slab in the middle of the space. 'I want you to try and dent it,' Victor says.

I turn to the metal. Debbie is sitting on top of it, barely there, wispy and empty. The wind rises, blasts into the metal but it stands firm, deflecting the air around it.

'Focus,' Victor shouts, and I stare at a point on the metal until my eyes hurt. I feel a needle in the back of my neck and cold surges through my body. I feel awake and alive and angry; the wind roars around the room, blasting into the metal but it is immovable. Victor is skidding across the floor, shouting, but I don't hear what he says, I want to defeat the metal. I want to break it, to bend it, to move it, but it is impossible. I throw gusts at it, create whirlwinds around it, try to break it open from the inside but it rises up from the ground. A tower of hard muscle. Looking down at me, eyes cloudy with the drink, watching as I fall to the floor.

CHAPTER
THIRTY-EIGHT

The sun is bright. I taste salt in the air, feel sand between my toes. Debbie is laughing in the distance. I look up and see her jumping over waves. She is young, just a little girl in a pink bathing suit without a care in the world.

Mum is near her, trousers rolled up to her knees, and she is looking at Debbie and smiling. She looks like the mum in the photograph on the mantelpiece.

I wobble to my feet and stagger towards the ocean, towards Mum. My legs are short and stubby, my fat, sandy fingers gripping a small plastic spade. Mum lifts me up, swings me onto her hip and as I rest my head on her shoulder she rests her hand on my head. I breathe in her smell, hold tight to her warm flesh, and she hums to me, slow and sweet.

The wind flows from the ocean, billows Mum's shirt into the air and the sky darkens as the sun disappears behind a huge black cloud. Mum holds out her hand to Debbie. Debbie runs out of the water and slips her wet fingers into Mum's dry ones. Mum leads her away from the shore, across the beach, where a choir is singing solemn, their robes billowing in the wind.

Mum goes stiff and sobs. I drop my spade and clutch her tighter, because I know if I lean back and look at her it won't be her; it'll be the other Mum, the sad one who always prays, the one that lives in our house, the bungalow. The one that died there.

CHAPTER THIRTY-NINE

I try and open my eyes but I can't; my eyelids are too heavy. The taste of bile fills my mouth and I feel sick.

'He's fighting it too much.' A strong voice cuts through the silence, the darkness. The director.

'He's making good progress.' Victor's words fall over me, echo in my ears. 'He has excellent control.'

'He's not ready to leave the compound.' Dr Epstein. I picture his sympathetic smile. The smile I hate.

'He's the perfect choice. He was in Tŷ Hapus with Griff.' Victor again.

'So were Madeline, Edward and Davis.'

'Paul would be more useful, and if you give him some freedom I think he will settle in faster.'

233

They are talking about me like I'm not here. A pain in my forehead swells and stabs deep into my brain. 'Who else are you planning to take?' The director's voice, stronger than the others.

'Didi and Aiden.'

'Go ahead. Do it today.' Heavy footfalls leave the room, a door swings shut, and Victor picks up my hand. I feel the needle pierce my skin and cold washes over me.

'Paul, can you hear me?' Dr Epstein lifts an eyelid and shines a bright light into my eye. I push him off and sit up, too hard, too fast. I expected to be restrained. Dr Epstein takes a step back so he is just behind Victor.

'You blacked out, Paul. You've been unconscious for an hour or so,' Victor smiles at me. 'You all right?'

'I think the dosage of your last injection may have been slightly too high,' Dr Epstein puts his torch back in his pocket, turns around and steps towards the door.

'Where are Angharad and Ric?' I call after him.

'Still undergoing assessment,' he says without turning around, and leaves the room.

'Do you remember Griff?' Victor asks.

I nod.

'We have located him and a few of us are going to find him, to bring him here. Would you like to come?'

I stare at him, unsure what to say. I feel torn in

different directions. I want to go, but it feels wrong. I want to leave, but not without Angharad and Ric.

'Come on,' Victor nods and I can't help it, I follow him.

'So what's Griff like?' Victor asks as we walk along the corridor.

'He doesn't say much.' I think back. I never heard him talk at all.

'We think he can make himself invisible.'

I remember Ric's explanation for Griff's disappearance; how I didn't believe him at the time. Everything is different now. I believe in impossible things.

Aiden and Didi are waiting at the double doors that lead outside. I feel air seeping through the cracks. I smell salt on the wind and I realise we must be near the sea.

Victor pushes the doors open and we walk into the light. It hits me hard, beautifully. The sour taste in my mouth disappears, I feel the breeze flow over my skin and for a moment I imagine I am free.

A wide, bleak estuary extends to the side of us. Wading birds are dotted across the sand, seagulls shriek in the air above. The sea crashes against rocks behind the building. A black van is parked in front of us, on a track that leads into woods in the distance.

Victor gets into the driving seat and Aiden sits next to him. I sit in the back with Didi. She is a slight girl with narrow eyes and colourful hair. She stares out of the window, her eyelids flickering as we slowly follow the track, through the woods, onto a main road and along the coast.

Aiden and Victor talk in the front. Every so often one of them asks me a question, tries to draw me into their conversation, but I don't respond. A feeling is gnawing at my stomach – the feeling that this wrong and I should do something but I can't help myself, I am not in control, but I know I don't want to make friends; I don't want to get comfortable. I remind myself I have to leave. I need to be with Debbie. The real Debbie.

'She's dead.' Didi turns to me. 'You have to let go, move on.'

Anger burns the back of my eyes. I am torn between ignoring her and shouting at her. It is none of her business. She doesn't know Debbie. She doesn't understand. I feel a breeze on the back of my neck and it distracts me because it has been so long since I felt Debbie's presence without the drugs.

The road takes us away from the coast; it gets smoother and wider until I realise we are on a motorway and the van is humming along monotonously, like Ric's droning chant in the sweat lodge. I stare out of the window, a grey world whizzing past in a blur. Hours pass in silence, although I think Victor and Aiden might be talking in the front. I don't know. I don't care. I am trying to find my own thoughts, the ones I am sure of; the ones where I know I have to leave and find Angharad and Ric and Debbie. Eventually the van slows, veers down a slip road, and we stop at a roundabout. Didi leans back and her eyelids flicker.

Victor drives slowly into a grey town, down grey streets, the rows of houses carving the sky into grey channels. No one speaks. I can hear Didi's eyelids flickering like tiny wings.

The van pulls to a stop in a backstreet. Long, crumbling walls extend either side of us, dilapidated wooden doors interspaced along. Bulging bin bags sit next to overflowing wheelie bins, some of them knocked over, spilling their contents onto the potholed tarmac road.

'He's not alone.' Didi opens her eyes wide. 'He's with three others, and they all have spirits.'

Aiden shakes his head. 'We need more people, then.'

'We can do this.' Victor steps out of the van and the others follow him. I climb out too, unsure what they expect me to do.

I look up and down the street. I could run away right now. Debbie would come back, I'm sure she would, without the pills and the injections she would come back and we could leave together. I look along the street and I want to run but something stops me. Maybe it's the thought of freeing Angharad and Ric. I wonder if I run away now, and Debbie comes back, I wonder if we could find Tŷ Eidolon again and break the others out. It's on an estuary by the sea … My heels rise from the floor and my fingers twitch as the thought of running becomes more real, but I still can't. The sour taste fills my mouth and I realise maybe it's the director in my head. Maybe that's why I can't run.

'Paul,' Victor is calling me in a loud whisper.

Didi has paused outside a cracked door with peeling green paint.

'You've got no idea who's in there with him or what powers they have.' Aiden looks at Victor and shakes his head.

'We know Griff is in there and he's invisible. He's the mission. Just Griff. Make a fire at the front of the house then come back round here. We'll get him as he leaves the building.'

'And if the others attack?'

'We defend ourselves.' Victor smiles and pulls one of my syringes out of his pocket and passes it to me.

Aiden jogs away, presumably round to the front of the house. Victor pushes the door open and beckons us inside. I'm not sure why I follow them, why I don't run. It's that feeling again, the one that has filled me for my days. I know I'm doing something wrong but I can't help myself, just like when I ran in the graveyard at Mum's funeral.

The garden is overgrown and neglected on a

scale I've never seen before. Waist-high grass and sprawling shrubs cover the small plot; rusty coils and spikes of metal poke out above the green, trying to claw their way out from the tangle of plants.

A narrow, slabbed path leads up to the house, barely visible in the shadow of the high wall to the side of it and beneath the spindly plants that droop over it. The slabs are broken, uneven, forced up by weeds growing from the cracks. We step along them towards a metal staircase that wavers up to the first floor of the house. The ground floor bay window beneath is mostly submerged by plant growth and covered with old newspapers stuck to the glass.

Victor pauses and turns to Didi behind him.

'They're all upstairs,' she nods, 'one girl, two boys.'

'Griff?'

She nods.

Victor injects himself and nods to me and I do the same; I inject the cold and Debbie appears on the steps, swinging her legs back and forth in slow motion. Her eyes are a deep, dark blur and her hair disappears into the air like smoke.

Smoke. Rising into the sky and drifting over the roof. Didi pulls me into the tangle of weeds and crouches down. I duck beside her, notice the litter woven into the vegetation at my feet.

There is no movement or noise from the house

for what seems like a long time. The paper-covered windows hide any activity. The smoke gets thicker and darker; the acrid smell of burning plastic fills my nose.

The rain starts suddenly; tightly packed needles flow from the sky in streams, striping the view and soaking every inch of clothing within moments.

'Don't disrupt the rain,' Didi whispers. 'We'll need it to spot Griff.'

It's then I realise Victor is making the rain. I look around but can't see him. A door at the top of the steps opens and smoke billows into the air, darkening as the rain wets it. Footfalls clang down the fire escape; a girl followed by two boys, the last one Griff.

Didi grips my arm. The girl and the first boy run past, and Didi pushes me into Griff. I stumble out of the weeds, crashing into him, and he stares at me, his eyes wide and startled like they were in Tŷ Hapus, and then he is gone in an instant.

I see his outline, an empty space where rain should be, but isn't, an invisible surface made visible only by the drops bouncing off it.

'I just want to talk.' It's like someone has put words into my mouth, speaking through me, and I taste the sourness and feel sick. I reach out a hand to Griff, but it's not like my hand, it's like someone else's and it feels so strange, but I am distracted by something wrapping round my leg.

I look down. The plants, the weeds, are rising up

my body, coiling around my limbs. Vines and tendrils are slapping onto my arms and pulling them down. I turn back to Griff but he is gone. A blur of empty space rushes past and is replaced by a girl, staring at me with bright green eyes. The plants immobilise me. I try and fight them off but they're like restraints. I turn my head and see Didi, covered in plants like me, then the tendrils rise up my neck and over the back of my head and I can't move at all.

The plants grow thicker, grip tighter, dig into my flesh, and anger rises inside me, hot and corrosive. The wind rises and raindrops swirl around, the vertical streams breaking up into a swirl of chaos. The door at the back of the garden slams and I hear shouting, but plants surround my ears and I can't make out the words. I am trapped, helpless. The wind surges and screams and loose plants are whipping around, but the ones holding onto me grip tighter, don't budge.

Suddenly, a flash of intense heat and orange light rolls across the ground like a wave onto a shore. My feet burn, my legs sting with pain, and the plants relax a little. Another wave of fire, and another, and the plants loosen, unwind and I struggle from their grasp, wrestle my way back onto the path, and see Aiden near the back door, circles of fire surging away from him into the garden. Victor is holding a small boy. He has his arms locked behind his back and the boy is squeezing his eyes shut and gritting his teeth and for a moment he reminds me of myself, and I am overwhelmed by the sour taste and the thought that this is wrong.

Something cracks and heaves behind me and I turn to see a fat tree root smash through the slabs. It curls around the girl with the green eyes and she steps onto it and it lifts her up towards the top of the wall. The girl steps onto the wall as the root catches fire and she looks down at me, her eyes reflecting flames. 'Why are you doing this? We're like you.'

'We want to help you,' Victor shouts from the back of the garden.

'You kill us,' the girl spits the words out. 'If we don't fit in, you kill us.' She turns to me, her eyes filled with fire and pain and anger, 'Where is Angharad? Have they killed her yet?'

Her words are like drops of detergent swirling in oil. Dispersing the sour taste in my mouth and the thoughts of the director in my mind, and the confusion, and whatever it is that is holding me trapped. I remember that I need to save Angharad and Ric; that I have to find out where they are. The thought occurs to me that it may be too late already.

The girl glances away towards Aiden; he has stepped towards her, flames rolling from his hands.

'Leave her. Look for Griff,' Didi shouts from among the plants and points to the back corner of

242

the garden where rain is swirling in chaotic eddies. 'Stop it, Paul!' she shouts, but I don't want to. I know they are like me; Griff, and the boy Victor is holding, and the girl with the green eyes. I see clearly they are like me, but I am trying to capture them like I was captured, so they can be taken away to be controlled by the director or cut up like Saeed.

The rain turns to hail, harder and faster, and I see it bouncing off Griff. His outline has become clear and Aiden must see it too, because he moves towards the space where the hail should be, flames roaring around him.

I don't want to be a part of this. I know I don't want to be a part of this anymore. I stare at the wall behind Griff and I think of the air in the cracks between the bricks, of the air in pockets inside the bricks and I see it warming, expanding, forcing the bricks apart.

Suddenly a chunk of wall blasts away, debris flies through the air and a gaping hole is left, another garden beyond it. The rainless space that is Griff hops into the hole and disappears. I turn around and see the girl has gone, but Victor is still holding the boy. He stares at me and the hail beats down harder, stinging my skin.

I throw all my anger at him. A blast of air flies into his chest and he reels back, loses his grip on the boy's arms, and the boy wriggles free. He seems to be glowing, pulsing with a strange white light, then all of a sudden there is a blinding flash of light, a deep, deafening boom, and an explosion of intense pressure; I think everyone simultaneously falls to the floor, and my ears are ringing and all I can see is white.

Griff is above me, his face a surface of nothing, a transparent curve of featureless features. He slips something into my pocket and disappears in a blur of empty movement. My ears keep ringing and my eyes can't focus, and although I try and sit up I can't move.

CHAPTER FORTY

There is a bright light just above my head. I feel the director stabbing into my brain with his thoughts and I push all my own away to the back of my mind. What I leave at the surface are the thoughts that were never really mine: that I want to stay, even though I know it is wrong; that Debbie is dead and I have to move on; that Ric and Angharad don't matter; that this place will be good for me; that I can be safe and learn to control my powers and be useful.

The pain stops and the light goes off.

'Wake him.' The director's voice.

A needle pierces my hand and cold washes over me.

'Paul?' Dr Epstein is leaning over me. 'Do you remember what happened?'

I sit up; wait for the room to come into focus.

The door opens and Victor walks in.

The director turns to him. 'Do you remember anything else?'

Victor shakes his head. 'It's all a blur. Griff was with a girl who could manipulate plants, and a boy. I had him but then he released some kind of shockwave. It knocked all of us out and they got away.' Victor looks at the floor.

I remember more. What the girl said, how it made me feel, breaking the wall, the shockwave, and Griff slipping something into my pocket. The memories flood into the front of my mind and I push them back, try and focus on only the thoughts that he wants me to have. The thoughts he pushed into my mind. The director stares at me and the pain returns. I think of the shockwave, only the shockwave, the strange, white light pulsing, the blinding flash, the deafening explosion, the ringing in my ears...

The director looks away and the pain stops. 'Return to training tomorrow.' He nods to Victor and leaves the room.

'I'll check you again tomorrow morning.' Dr Epstein turns to leave but I call after him.

'Where are Angharad and Ric?'

He looks back at me and gives me his sympathetic smile. The smile I hate. 'I'm afraid they won't be staying with us, Paul. They're both scheduled to be released.'

My heart beats faster. 'You're going to operate on them?'

Dr Epstein shakes his head. 'Ric is being transferred to a mental health hospital. He is simply schizophrenic, with no discernible powers. He needs a different kind of help to what we offer here.'

They still don't know about Ric, about what he can do, about the things he can project. 'What about Angharad?'

Dr Epstein looks past me, at the wall behind me. 'As I said, Paul, it is a simple operation. Minimal risk. Her voices will be gone and she can start a new life on the outside. It's her choice.'

My fists flush with heat and I clench them. 'Angharad wouldn't choose that. She is happy with her voices. They're her sisters.'

'It's the only option for her, Paul. Her condition is different from yours; it is exceedingly difficult to control. Unfortunately, we cannot offer her anything else.' Dr Epstein looks back to me, looks me in the eyes. 'She will be fine. We will help her start a new life on the outside. She'll be happy.' He smiles, turns and leaves.

'Come on,' Victor says, 'I'll walk you back to your dorm.'

I follow him in silence, thoughts and plans hurtling around my head. I need to find them, and I need to get them out of here. Tonight.

'When can I be in control of my medication?' I

ask Victor.

'As soon as the Director approves. I'll ask him tomorrow if you like.'

I nod. Tomorrow is not soon enough.

The dorm is quiet, the boys already in bed. Victor says goodnight and I sit on my bed, pull the piece of paper out of my pocket and stare at it.

It is a rough sketch of a girl with short hair lying slumped on a gravelly beach, a cliff behind her, a pier in the distance. I see circles through the paper, turn it over and see the symbol, Ric's tattoo, of the concentric circles being smashed by the lightning bolt. I realise the lightning is Angharad. The circles are Eventual Eidolon. I have to free her. If I save her she will stop them, just like Ric said the very first time we met.

I look at the sketch again, of the girl on the beach. Ric talked about this, too. He said we would leave Angharad on a beach and the others would find her. I push away the memory of what he said after that.

'Paul?' Davis whispers from the bed next to me. 'Did you find Griff?'

'No.' I shake my head. I move to him, kneel down beside him. 'Davis.'

'What?' He looked concerned.

'They are going to operate on Angharad's brain. To take her voices away.'

Tyrone slips out of his bed and creeps over to us. 'They are going to do what?'

248

'Operate on Angharad to take her voices away.'

'Why?' Tyrone asks. 'Why don't they let her train with us?'

'Because they can't control her. All of us here, we're all being controlled with drugs and by the director.' I look at them. They must know it's true. They must feel him in their heads, too.

They just stare at me, silent.

'I want to get her out,' I whisper, 'her and Ric.'

Tyrone shakes his head, 'You can't –'

'I have to try.' I look at them both, wonder if they would help.

Neither of them says anything and I don't have to be a mind reader to know what they're thinking. They like it here. They don't want to jeopardise their new lives by getting on the wrong side of the Director.

'Maybe I'm confused,' I say, 'tired after today.' I move back to my bed and get under the covers and wait.

I wait until all the boys have been asleep for hours, until nothing but slow and steady breaths murmur through the dorm, and then I creep to the door.

The corridor is empty. I look along it, to the door at the other end. How far could I get before someone came? What could I do if someone did come?

I wish Debbie was here. I can't feel her at all.

I step quietly along the corridor, my heart

racing. The door ahead of me opens and my heart stops. It's Victor. He walks towards me and smiles.

'Can I help you, Paul?'

I hesitate for a moment, unsure, and then I throw a punch. It connects with his jaw and he staggers back. It starts raining, fat heavy drops that fall faster and harder. I step forwards and punch him again and he falls to his knees. The rain turns to hail, and the hailstones get bigger and sharper; they sting my face and hands. I look down at Victor and raise my fist again.

He grabs my leg, and where his hand connects, just below my knee, intense cold burns through my flesh and bone, freezes it, cripples it. The pain is intense. I stifle a scream and punch him again and he falls to the floor. As he falls he kicks out and connects with my ankle. It feels like daggers of ice pierce my skin and embed into my foot. I grit my teeth, pull my leg back and kick it into his abdomen as hard as I can. I expect my leg to shatter like glass, but it doesn't. The kick winds Victor and he folds into himself, trying to breathe.

I reach into his breast pocket and pull out the syringes, fumble until I see a red one with his name on it, and I stab it into his arm. His muscles relax and he gasps for air. I find his other red syringe, and I stab him with that too, and he closes his eyes, out cold.

The door to the dorm opens and I turn around, struggle to my feet. The leg Victor froze is useless, unresponsive. Hasan moves into the corridor. He looks at Victor behind me and frowns.

Flames flicker between us and I feel their warmth growing. I look through the remaining syringes, find the green one with my name on it, and stab it into my leg. Icy water flows over me and I see Debbie, floating, like she did in the pit.

Debbie?

'I'm here, Paul.' Her voice is weak, her mouth doesn't move. She is faint but the wind picks up. It moves the flames between me and Hasan; blows them towards him. He steps back and shouts to the others in the dorm.

Thick, green fog billows out of the door and I see the shapes of the boys within it. The wind picks up, blows the fog down the corridor, but it doesn't clear; it just spreads further.

I feel a hand on my elbow and I turn, fist raised, but it's Tyrone I see in the fog, and I can't hit him. He pulls me back against the wall, and I feel the floor rising, tilting, the walls bending. The whole corridor seems to be crumpling.

'Push them back into the dorm,' he whispers near my ear.

I throw the wind at the boys, focus it towards to the dorm and I see them amidst the fog, falling back. I step forwards and grab Davis, pull him next to me as the wind pushes the rest of them into the dorm.

The door slams and bends into the wall, until it

is mangled and the boys are trapped on the other side. The green fog clears and the wind whips around us.

I turn to Davis. 'Can you show me where they are?'

Davis nods and pulls a green syringe from his pocket. He injects himself and looks around, finding his shadows along the crumpled walls.

'This way,' he nods, and I follow him along the corridor, Tyrone close behind. We go through the doors and start climbing the stairs. Davis pauses and turns to me. 'Akim is at the top.' I step ahead of Davis and carry on up the stairs, a gale blowing ahead of me.

Akim is standing, gripping the stair rail, leaning into the wind. He looks at me, squinting, and I feel myself lift off the floor. I push more wind at him, throw it at him in gusts and whirls, but he stands firm and I keep rising off the floor.

A metallic creak echoes along the stair rail and it tears off the wall, bends towards Akim, and he topples backwards. I suddenly fall, plummet down and smash into the metal steps. I gasp and try to lift myself up. My leg, the one Victor froze, keeps buckling. I look up to the top of the stairs. Tyrone is there, standing over Akim, who is now wrapped in the stair rail. Davis grabs my hand, helps me to my feet, and we carry on up the stairs, past Akim, and through the next set of doors into a corridor.

'Ric's in there,' Davis points to a door on the

left side. 'You don't have long; lots of them are coming.'

Tyrone steps in front of me and stares at the door. It folds, rips from its hinges, and falls to the floor with a bang. Ric is laughing behind it. He looks pale and shaky; he reminds me of Tom from my dream.

'I knew you were coming,' he smiles. 'Chief –'

'We have to get Angharad out,' I shout. 'People are coming, now.'

A scream from the corridor deafens me. I recognise the noise; Max. I cover my ears and hold my head to keep it from bursting. The noise stops and my ears start ringing. I run into the corridor and see Max standing over Tyrone, who is unconscious on the floor. I throw the wind at him and he flies backwards and hits the doors behind him. Ric runs after him, fists raised, and I pick up Tyrone and carry him to Davis, who is crouched near another door, further along the corridor.

'Angharad's in there,' Davis nods at the door.

I put Tyrone down and stare at the door. I focus the wind into the centre of it. I think about Angharad on the other side. I have to get her out. There will be no second chances.

I imagine a vortex, the centre of a hurricane, forming inside the door, twisting it, tearing it. The door warps, the hinges snap and the door falls to the floor.

Angharad is lying on a bed, eyes closed. As I

step towards her something sharp pierces my neck and I fall to the floor. Everything is quiet. The air is still. Debbie is gone.

I look up and see the Director, his face stern, his eyes staring into mine, and pain spreads across my forehead. I look away. I tense all my muscles and I kick back, try to swipe his legs out from under him but he stands firm. The pain in my head swells, throbs; I scream and close my eyes. I am overwhelmed by the pain, the frustration, the anger. I have to stop him. I have to get us out of here, but I don't know how anymore.

CHAPTER FORTY-ONE

The lights go out. There is complete darkness for a moment, then a blinding electrical flash shoots from behind me and crashes into the Director and the pain stops. I hear him fall to the floor and the smell of burning hair fills the room.

The lights flicker and I see the Director on the floor, holding his chest and gasping for air. He looks up at me, and at Angharad, and the pain splits my head again, sharper, harder, like something is being driven into my skull. I try and kick him but my legs won't move, try and punch him but my arms are pinned to my sides. I hear Angharad scream but I can't move; I can't do anything. I feel like I am going to burst.

Lightning shoots across the room again. Continuous, blinding, jagged streams of it arc out of Angharad's hands and stab into the Director. She is screaming, louder and louder; her pale face twisted in anger. The Director is shaking and the pain in my head subsiding.

Ric runs in and stops and shields his eyes from the light. He makes his way towards Angharad, stepping around the Director and over me. He reaches her, puts his arm around her waist, and she stops screaming. The lightning disappears, darkness falls, and Angharad dips towards the floor. Ric catches her, lifts her into his arms, and a flame appears behind them.

I stare at the flame. It is a burning torch. An arm is holding it, a face behind it; a Native American wearing a feather headdress. A warrior, a chief. Ric carries Angharad to the door and the chief follows them, lighting the way with his torch. They step over the Director, now lying unconscious on the floor, and I follow them into the corridor.

I help Davis to his feet and lift Tyrone up, carry him over my shoulder. The doors ahead of us open and uniforms file into the corridor. Ric starts chanting, slow and steady, faster and louder, and warriors start appearing between us and the uniforms. Native American warriors, with bows and arrows, spears, axes and clubs. As they appear they run along the corridor, yelling. I stare at them; Ric's voices, his spirits.

Some uniforms fall back, others run towards the warriors. In an instant there is chaos; shouts and war cries, smoke and fire and rain. A group of warriors appear and encircle us as we move along the corridor. Beyond them I see uniforms staring, confused. The warriors throw weapons that reappear in their hands instantly. Some leave the circle to charge towards a uniform, but when they do another appears in their place.

It takes me a minute to realise that for all the battle around us, the uniforms are not getting hurt. The warriors can't touch them. Their weapons are an illusion. They are all just an illusion.

Agatha must realise this at the same time as me and she runs at us. She passes right through the warriors and barges into Ric. He stumbles and nearly drops Angharad. I step in front of them and spin Tyrone towards her, so his legs connect with the side of her head. She ducks and jabs at my ribs. The force of her punch is enormous, superhuman. I feel my ribs give way and I buckle downwards, and Tyrone falls over my head. Agatha kicks me, I hear a crack and my arm explodes in pain. I look up at her; she is raising her fist, aiming for my head.

I think about Debbie. I won't lose her again. It doesn't matter that the Director injected me; I can beat his medicines. I can bring Debbie now and she can help me. I think about the air between me and Agatha's fist. Debbie is in that air; she is everywhere, and she will help me.

The fist stops moving, Agatha pushes it towards me but it won't come any closer. The air between us pushes back, her fist moves back, the wind surges towards her; she falls, hits the wall and slides to the floor.

I pick up Tyrone and we move forward, surrounded by warriors. The wind rushes ahead of us, pushing the uniforms back. I don't know how many uniforms fall back, how many we pass, but no one else fights us, no one gets close. The warriors lead us through doors, down stairs, along a corridor, and finally to the hallway, where the large double doors are the only thing between us and the outside. I feel the cold night air behind it seeping through the cracks.

I throw the wind at the doors and they swing open. I feel something pulling on my sleeve. I look down and see Davis staring up at me; my heart sinks. I can see he wants to stay. I put Tyrone down, see his eyes flicker. I slap his face gently, call his name.

'Tyrone, are you coming with us?'

He opens his eyes and I see it there, too. He doesn't want to leave. Neither him, nor Davis. I feel defeated.

'Are you coming with us?' I ask again, but I already know the answer.

I turn and follow Ric, who is carrying Angharad, still surrounded by warriors, out of the door, and into the salty black night. I hear the door creak, close and bend behind us as I follow Ric, away from the building, down a slope, and towards the ocean.

CHAPTER FORTY-TWO

The warriors fade away, disappear into the darkness. Ric stumbles down the slope, his breathing heavy. I can hear the ocean washing onto rocks ahead of us.

Ric picks up speed, skids onto a muddy shore and jogs along it.

'Ric?' I catch up with him, try to see his face, but it is too dark. There is no moon, no stars.

'Ric?'

He mutters something, laughs, stops and spins his head around.

'Ric?'

He carries on jogging.

I stay with him, following him along the shore. He keeps changing pace; stopping, listening, laughing, shouting, jogging, running, but he never hears me. He is talking to his voices, spirits I can't see, in a language I can't understand.

The ground changes, becomes rocky and slippery. Ric stumbles his way over the rocks, chanting and muttering. I offer to carry Angharad but he ignores me, shouts at one of his voices and jogs further into the darkness.

We walk for hours. The horizon slowly emerges from the darkness; a stormy grey sky hangs heavy over a black ocean. I look at Ric's face, twisted by shadows and emotion. He is sweating, agitated; his eyes darting round, his mouth trying to have ten conversations at once.

'Ric?' I try again, put my hand on his shoulder and he stops and looks at me. His eyes look into mine, but I'm not sure he sees me. His eyes are wild, confused. They are full of excitement, fear, anger and sadness; they remind me of Debbie's eyes, and I feel scared, cold in my chest.

We round a peninsula and there is a pier in the distance, lit by a single row of weak orange lights. Ric stops, sets Angharad on the floor, and runs along the gravel shore towards it.

'Ric!' I shout, but he ignores me and keeps running. I pick up Angharad and run after him, but he gets further and further away from me.

By the time I reach the end of the gravelly beach, Ric is nearly out of sight. He has climbed the rocky cliffs ahead and is jogging towards the pier beyond them.

I set Angharad down at the base of cliffs, in a small sheltered cave, and climb up after him.

I run along the pier, my footsteps resonating along the wooden planks, echoing above the sound of the waves. The line of orange lights leads towards the ocean, to the horizon beyond. The sky is grey and cloudy, the sea dark and restless. I can't see Ric. I am nearly at the end of the pier but I can't see him.

I reach the end, put my hands on the railings, and lean over the edge. The sea below is churning, white froth folding into thick, dark water.

'He's gone, Paulie.' Debbie is sitting on the railings, swinging her legs back and forth.

SHUT UP.

I run alongside the railings and keep looking over the edge, but there is no sign of Ric.

'He's gone.'

SHUT UP.

Panic wells in my chest and air catches in my throat, swells and blocks it.

'You couldn't have done anything, Paulie.' Debbie jogs backwards in front of me.

SHUT UP.

I fall to the floor, look through the gaps between the wooden planks of the boardwalk, and see the waves crashing and arguing below. I put my head on the planks and close my eyes.

Please, I think. *Please. No.*

Everything goes quiet and I feel soft and heavy, like I am sinking into the floor. I hear Debbie singing, beneath me, above me, and around me.

Show me peace
Amid the roar
Show me peace, show me peace
Find me waves
Along the shore
Show me peace, show me peace.

I stand and look around, but I can't see her. She carries on singing, and Ric's voice joins hers, but I can't see him either, and his voice, like Debbie's, is coming from everywhere.

Blow across the open sky
Show me peace before I die
Come for me with gentle song
Speak of good and not of wrong
Show me peace
Among the waves
Show me peace, show me peace
Show me peace
Among the graves

Show me peace, show me peace.

'*SHUT UP!*' I shout it into the wind. '*SHUT UP!*'

Debbie appears in front of me, floating, like she did in the pit. She sings, soft and sweet.

Show me peace
Among the waves.

'*THERE IS NO PEACE AMONG THE WAVES*,' I scream at her. '*JUST BLACK AND DEATH AND NOTHING. JUST A WASTE OF LIFE.*'

'How can you say that, Paulie?' Debbie stops singing and looks at me. 'I'm here.'

'*NO*,' I shout at her. '*YOU'RE NOT.*' I reach for her and my hand trembles. It doesn't want to move forwards. '*YOU'RE DEAD.*' My eyes sting. My fingers hover above her cheek.

She's a memory, an imprint, a ghost; I don't know, but she's not real. She's not alive.

'*YOU'RE IN MY HEAD*,' I shout it at her, tense my muscles, and drop my fingers onto her cheek and there is no cheek. My hand falls to my side and Debbie is gone.

I run along the pier again; keep looking into the water. The wind picks up, blowing off the sea, filled with salt that stings my skin.

The singing, the voices, are drowned out by the roar of the wind and it gets stronger and louder until all I can hear is the wind, and it pushes me back across the pier.

Waves crash below and throw up spray that spatters the boardwalk, and the wind gets stronger still until the boards are shaking and the railings creaking.

I fall to the floor and I close my eyes. I squeeze them shut and I scream, louder than I ever have before. I scream and scream, until I feel like I am going to burst and then darkness surrounds me and everything goes quiet.

EPILOGUE

'Wakey wakey, Paul.'

I open my eyes and a barcode of light and shadow moves across my vision. It's Debbie, running her hands across the bars on the window.

I've been back in young offenders for eight months. I chose to come here; I am in control. I could be released soon. Early, on account of my good behaviour.

'Paulie?'

Debbie looks real, but she's not. I turn away from her. Good behaviour means I ignore her. I keep my voices secret for now, like Ric used to; because I don't want to go back to Tŷ Hapus, or Tŷ Eidolon – the places they say don't exist.

They say none of what happened was real; the police, the wardens, the case workers, the psychologists; they say there was no Ric, no Angharad, no Tyrone and no Davis. My case worker even took me to Tŷ Hapus once; to show me what a nice place it is, that it's not burned down, that there is no Dr Stuart and no Dr Epstein.

Madeline was there; she said she remembered me, but not the others. Pam was there too, but she didn't talk to me, she simply slipped through a door when she saw me, holding her crucifix.

They say there is no Tŷ Eidolon; they say it was all a delusion, but I know they are lying. I know what is real. I am in control.

'Spar with me, Paul.' Debbie jumps around in front of me. Light and shadows play on her face.

I turn away from her. She's not real.

'You're no fun anymore, Paulie.' She skips to the window, strums on the bars, and I squeeze my eyes shut.

Something slides under the door and I stare at it. A piece of paper, a folded note. I pick it up and open it. Inside is a drawing, a sketch; concentric circles are fractured, smashed by a jagged line with an arrow head, like a bolt of lightning. The lights flicker off and I go to the window, watch her walking away.

A gentle breeze flows over me and I smile, because I know what I am going to do when I get out of here.

With Special Thanks to
The Accent YA Editor Squad

Aishu Reddy

Alice Brancale

Amani Kabeer-Ali

Anisa Hussain

Barooj Maqsood

Ellie McVay

Grace Morcous

Katie Treharne

Miriam Roberts

Rebecca Freese

Sadie Howorth

Sanaa Morley

Sonali Shetty

With Special Thanks to

The Accent YA Blog Squad

Alix Long;

Anisah Hussein;

Anna Ingall;

Annie Starkey;

Becky Freese;

Becky Morris;

Bella Pearce;

Beth O'Brien;

Caroline Morrison;

Charlotte Jones;

Charnell Vevers;

Claire Gorman;

Daniel Wadey;

Darren Owens;

Emma Hoult;

Fi Clark;

Heather Lawson;

James Briggs

With Special Thanks to

The Accent YA Blog Squad

James Williams;

Joshua A.P;

Karen Bultiauw;

Katie Lumsden;

Katie Treharne;

Kieran Lowley;

Laura Metcalfe;

Lois Acari;

Maisie Allen;

Mariam Khan;

Philippa Lloyd;

Rachel Abbie;

Rebecca Parkinson;

Savannah Mullings-Johnson;

Sofia Matias;

Sophia;

Toni Davis

INDIGO'S DRAGON

SOFI CROFT

Indigo lives in the Lake District, and spends his time exploring the mountains he loves. An unexpected parcel arrives containing a first aid kit inside his grandfather's satchel. Indigo's curiosity is raised as he looks through his grandfather's notebook to discover drawings of mythical creatures.

Strange things begin to happen and Indigo finds himself treating an injured magpie-cat, curing a cockatrice of its death-darting gaze, and defending a dragon. Indigo realises he must uncover the secrets his family have kept hidden, and travels alone to the Polish mountains to search for his grandfather and the truth.

INDIGO'S DEMONS

SOFI CROFT

Indigo's life is out of control. He has grown wings and can breathe fire, and fears he may be turning into a dragon altogether. His grandfather has gone, leaving behind a sanctuary full of monsters that are becoming increasingly dangerous, and although his uncle has arrived to help, Indigo begins to suspect that he is keeping secrets from him.

Unsure of what else to do, Indigo goes in search of his friend, Rue, hoping she can help, but instead he finds a castle full of demons – ruthless killers that may be more dangerous than anything in his life, yet encountering them may help Indigo understand himself.

THE DEEPEST CUT
natalie flynn

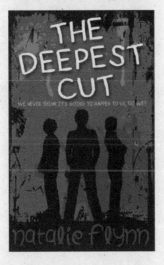

'You haven't said a single word since you've been here. Is it on purpose?' I tried to answer David but I couldn't ... my brain wanted to speak but my throat wouldn't cooperate...

Adam blames himself for his best friend's death. After attempting suicide, he is put in the care of a local mental health facility. There, too traumatized to speak, he begins to write notebooks detailing the events leading up to Jake's murder, trying to understand who is really responsible and cope with how needless it was as a petty argument spiralled out of control and peer pressure took hold.

For more information about **Sofi Croft**

and other **Accent YA** titles

please visit

www.accentya.com